THE PREDATOR™
HUNTERS AND HUNTED

THE OFFICIAL MOVIE PREQUEL

THE PREDATOR™

HUNTERS AND HUNTED

AN ORIGINAL NOVEL BY JAMES A. MOORE

BASED ON THE SCREENPLAY WRITTEN BY
FRED DEKKER & SHANE BLACK

BASED ON THE CHARACTERS CREATED BY
JIM THOMAS & JOHN THOMAS

DIRECTED BY SHANE BLACK

TITAN BOOKS

THE PREDATOR: HUNTERS AND HUNTED
Print edition ISBN: 9781785654268
E-book edition ISBN: 9781785657931

Published by Titan Books
A division of Titan Publishing Group Ltd
144 Southwark Street, London SE1 0UP

First edition: July 2018
10 9 8 7 6 5 4 3 2 1

A CIP catalogue record for this title is available from the British Library.

Printed and bound in the United States.

1

The Central American heat was stifling, and the humidity made it feel as if they were working in a sauna, but they were used to that and worse. It was all part of the training.

None of the Reapers blinked. Ever. Not when it came to combat. Not when it came to doing their duty. They were hardcore and they were dangerous and they knew it.

Officially, they did not exist. The Reapers were strictly off the books, especially for the military. They had to be, because, officially, their targets did not exist. The military frowned on the idea of trying to hunt extraterrestrials.

They had trained together for months—ever since they'd been hand-picked by General Woodhurst and the man who was directly responsible for their specialized training, Roger Elliott of the CIA. They were as well-oiled a machine as Erik Tomlin had ever known, and not one of them considered questioning his orders.

Their targets for this mission were of a distinctly terrestrial nature—more than a dozen men, perhaps as many as twenty, with serious hardware and a few too many contacts in the drug trade. Though not as exotic as the prey the team was being trained to address, these "importers" would allow them to work out the details of how best to work as a team.

So they were in the middle of nowhere, dropped off in the darkest part of the night. There were no street lights in the area. Hell, there was only one road, and it was little more than a dirt trail. The foliage was heavy and laden with moisture, the insects were everywhere, and the chances of being spotted depended entirely on whether or not their targets had any dogs, because sure as hell they didn't have the advanced technology that would help them identify incoming enemies.

There was no barking. There were no dogs.

That was a nice bonus.

"Time to do our civic duty, boys," Tomlin said, and just like that everyone was go. They moved with utter silence, sliding closer and closer to their objective—a Quonset hut. All of the intelligence that had been gathered indicated that their targets would be inside. Its bay door was open, but only a dim light shone from within.

Next to him, Hyde moved along, as cold a man as Tomlin had ever seen in action. In lieu of a firearm he was carrying two very long knives. He started moving ahead of the rest, working as a scout, prepared to take out anyone he saw. Hyde specialized in wetwork. Hell, according to a few of the guys he got off on the kill. Didn't matter. As long as he got the job done—and he did— Tomlin was fine with that.

The rest of the team crouched in the underbrush, ready to act, but they waited, as did Tomlin, for a signal from Hyde.

Then the rain started. Three hot fat drops of warm water splashed across Tomlin's helmet, and then the heavens unleashed a furious deluge of the stuff. There was no in-between—from nothing to a fury of rain and wind. The sudden roar of the downpour would help to mask their presence.

Just seconds after it started, they all saw Hyde's signal. Emerging from the shadows they went for the open bay door, moving silently and swiftly. Taking up positions to either side of the entrance, they saw no one—at least not yet—and slipped inside.

The inside of the place was a large collection of boxes on pallets, all stacked in neat, precise islands. Tomlin signaled for the Reapers to go in three separate groups, and they followed his orders without a sound. Two soldiers spilled away in each direction, sticking close to the shadows. No telling when they'd have company.

Up ahead of him Tomlin spotted a shadow breaking from the twilight darkness inside the place. There were lights, but only enough to illuminate the passageways created by the towering pallets of supplies and finished product. The shadow was Hyde, on the move. He took three steps, held up a hand to still them, and then slipped into another pool of darkness just before two men in jeans and black t-shirts moved into view.

There had been no footsteps, so their boots must have boasted a polyurethane outsole, Tomlin guessed. He tensed, prepared to fight them if he had to, but he needn't have bothered. Hyde stepped in close to the one on the left and drew him backward even as his partner started to say something. He was looking in the opposite direction.

Not a sound indicated the disappearance of the first man. When there was no response his companion stopped and looked around, puzzled but not yet alarmed. He opened his mouth to speak when Hyde emerged again from the shadows, clamping a hand over his mouth, his blade silencing the guy with a single stroke across the throat.

Grabbing the body before it could fall, he lowered it without a sound and began to drag it into the darkness.

Then things went sideways.

Another of the cartel members came out of the darkness and stumbled across Hyde just as he was dragging the corpse across the concrete floor. The guy let out a screech of shock before anyone could react, and a moment after that there were several voices calling out.

There were no alarm bells, no klaxon sirens. There was just a sudden gathering of men armed with assault rifles who wanted to make sure their business was left alone. But their movements were clumsy, disorganized, with a hint of panic—the men were amateurs in comparison to the Reapers. However, though they lacked training, they had serious firepower.

Worse, there were substantially more than twenty of them.

Even so, it was no contest. As the enemy scattered in every direction, shots began to ring out one at a time, producing a loud *crack* that echoed through the space, and the random burst of automatic rifle fire when one of the drug dealers panicked and started shooting at shadows. When that happened there would be a flashing light that left the darkness that much blacker.

A trio of the thugs approached Tomlin's hiding place. Three well-placed bullets from his standard-issue Beretta M9 put them down before they could utter a sound.

Occasional screams accompanied the gunfire. Before the Reapers were done the body count was over thirty. They took the site in less than five minutes. As silence again filled the hut, Tomlin gestured and his men scoured the place, following a pre-established search pattern. Once they were certain that there were no survivors, Strand went to work.

Tomlin moved quickly past the lab and located the main office exactly where their intelligence said it would be. None of the files were locked, so it was easy for him to find what he needed, pack it away, and get the hell out. Trotting back through the stacks of crates, he signaled the rest to follow, and they sprinted back into the jungle.

Four minutes after the last body was dropped and the intelligence was collected, the entire hut went up in a deafening burst of flames.

The Reapers left the area with time to spare. Not knowing if there were patrols that would have been alerted by the explosion, they moved through the underbrush without saying a word. The rain had eased up a little, though it was still a steady downpour. Despite his high-tech headgear, Tomlin could only see one or two of the men at a time, but he knew they were all there.

Their appointed pickup site was close by, and they

didn't encounter any opposition. If there had been patrols, most likely they ran like hell as soon as the Quonset hut went up like the Fourth of July.

↗ ↗ ↗

The plane ride was smooth and steady, but none of the Reapers paid it much attention. They had better things to do with their time than worry about turbulence.

Tomlin began sorting his equipment and looked around the interior of the plane. None of the Reapers wore rank or insignias of any sort. That was part of what they were and what they did. For this mission they were on loan to the CIA, which seemed entirely logical, given the covert nature of what they did.

"You in there, Tomlin?" There was a rapping on his helmet, Devon Hill's voice cut through Tomlin's thoughts, and he looked toward his second in command.

"Where else would I be?" He smiled as he said it.

Hill smiled back, but there was no warmth to it.

"Mars? Hell, I dunno. You tell me." Hill was a solid man. His dark-brown body was toned from obsessive exercise and hard training, and he was capable of running fifteen miles with full gear and hardly breaking a sweat. Like all of the Reapers he took his regimen very seriously. He regarded Tomlin with a hawk's intensity, and the squad leader knew what it felt like to be a rabbit. Then the guy turned back to his own gear.

A former Navy Seal, Hill wanted to be in command, Tomlin knew. Not because he thought Tomlin wasn't capable, but because he was obsessed with being the best. To him, taking command would confirm that he had succeeded. It wasn't personal.

Tomlin still felt like prey.

"Got some chatter coming in," Orologas called out. "Sounds like Woodhurst might be back. Wonder if we still have jobs."

"We'll find out when we get back," Tomlin said, and he shrugged. "No sense wasting time on it now." Truth be told, he wasn't particularly concerned. General Woodhurst was in charge of the Reapers and everything else at Project Stargazer. There had been talk of budget cuts, talk of dismantling the program, and constant chatter about how many things could go wrong since the day the program was started. So far none of it had happened, to the point that he just tuned it all out.

They were still there because Woodhurst was smart. He'd found ways to make work happen, like the mission they'd just completed—and quite successfully. Officially, they hadn't gone into Central America. Officially, they hadn't taken down a cartel that was working out new and improved ways to get stupid college kids addicted to hard drugs. Officially, the Reapers didn't exist—and yet they'd just been to Nicaragua, had just eliminated a pack of hostiles, and destroyed one of the more active labs making the newest version of synthetic cocaine.

His equipment properly stowed, Tomlin found a seat and studied the rest of his team. In addition to Hill, who'd been pulled from the Seals for the Reapers, there was Elmore Strand—hands down the most uptight guy that Tomlin had ever met. He made Hill look relaxed.

Strand specialized in explosives. He could make them. He could defuse them. He could probably assemble and disassemble a nuclear warhead, not that he'd had any reason... so far. Cool as an ice cube in a bad situation, and Tomlin had never seen anyone more efficient. When it came time to relax, though, he was volatile. Most likely to get into a fistfight over nothing. Maybe the two things were related. The man could handle the pressure as long as he had to, and then he needed to vent.

The demolitions specialist kept his head shaved and he was clean-shaven. Though relatively short, and thinner than most of the team, he worked out as hard as anyone else, was adept at hand-to-hand, and was a skilled marksman besides.

Still, Hill had said it best. The man had dead eyes.

As frightening as Strand was, Jermaine Hyde was worse. Covert ops meant wetwork, and Hyde was their specialist. There had been occasions where the man had gone in ahead of the rest of the team and basically finished the job before they reached him. Not only did he excel at killing quietly, the man appeared to enjoy his work—a bit too much for Tomlin's comfort.

Hyde was long and lean, his muscles corded and his skin unblemished by any tattoos. Most of the group had some sort of ink, but Hyde didn't like the notion at all. It might have been a moot point, though. If there was a man with darker skin, Tomlin had never met him. If there was any man who talked less, the same stood true. Hyde answered questions, and now and again he even cracked a joke, but it was rare for him to speak except to acknowledge an order.

On the opposite end of the spectrum there was Kyle Pulver.

Pulver was a freckled mess—his skin didn't tan, it burned, and when it was done burning, freckles came in like scars. He had an easygoing smile, and was almost constantly cracking jokes, though only when they were done with a mission. No practical jokes. Those didn't happen. Men like the Reapers might laugh at a firecracker going off, or they might kill a few people while trying to figure out where the gunfire was coming from.

Pulver had finished with his equipment and was shuffling cards with a skill that would have made most Vegas dealers nervous. He looked up at Tomlin and nodded. Beyond that there was no acknowledgment. As far as Pulver was concerned, the mission wasn't done until they settled at the base. On that they all agreed.

Dmitri Orologas was their communications specialist. He spoke too many languages to count, and had the technical skills to rebuild a radio with ease. His hair was kept close and his face was dark with stubble that seemed to appear seconds after he shaved it. His broad features were normally set in a remarkably neutral expression, and he seemed happiest when he was actively translating one language to another.

Tomlin had failed high school Spanish and never looked back, so he was grateful to have someone who actually liked the idea of knowing what everyone was saying at any given moment.

Somewhere in all the files Stargazer possessed, there was a sound bite that was allegedly from an alien speaking in a language from another world. Tomlin had heard it, but all it sounded like to him was gurgling and a few weird clicking sounds. Orologas had heard it too, and it drove him crazy. He was still trying to translate it into something that made sense, but so far, no luck.

Orologas liked to talk, but hated idle chatter. He was also an excellent cook and a decent field medic. At the moment he was talking with Edward King, their combat medic. King was way beyond that, though—he was a surgeon. He was also a soldier who followed orders with the best of them. As the two of them talked, it sounded as if Orologas was helping King learn a second language. Tomlin was pretty sure it was French, but didn't feel like asking.

Locked into his seatbelt like a good little frequent flyer, the last member of the team was Steve Burke. He was the heavy artillery man, after Pulver. He was also the team's security lead.

Hill looked his way and scowled as he rubbed at his shoulder. He'd taken down a man who outweighed him by almost a hundred pounds and he'd done it well, but a few muscles got pulled in the process.

"I know this is supposed to be good exercise," he growled loudly enough to be heard over the engines, "to prepare us for what we've been hired to do, but I've got to say, taking on a bunch of drug-dealing assholes—and inept ones at that—doesn't seem much like a serious challenge."

"Well, it's better than playing video games," Tomlin replied.

Hill snorted at that, and grinned. The first four months of training had been just that, combat via virtual reality games. It had been fun, had educated them in the use of a number of new weapons, and had familiarized them with a wide variety of combat environments and scenarios— not all of them on the surface of the earth. But it hadn't really done much for honing their physical reflexes or increasing their ability to work together.

As much as he appreciated the successful end to a mission, Tomlin didn't much like doing black ops. That wasn't what he'd signed up for, but he also saw the benefits of being "loaned out" to the CIA and other groups. The Reapers did good work—productive, beneficial work—and they got to learn more about being a cohesive operation. As a bonus, they stopped a few bastards from selling shit in the US. He had a little brother and two sisters. If he could make sure they stayed away from that sort of crap, all the better.

"I'm just sayin' I wish we'd find someone who makes us work up a sweat," Hill said without a hint of irony, "and do what we're supposed to be doing."

"Same here." Tomlin nodded. Several of the others did the same.

The weather outside was getting rougher, and their transport lurched, then dropped a few hundred feet. Those who were strapped in just relaxed and enjoyed it. Those who weren't grabbed for the nearest handhold and rode it out. There were a couple of grunts, but no one showed any real concern.

They approached southern Georgia, where the countryside around them was flat and wet, and steaming hot. According to the app on his phone the temperature was ninety-eight degrees Fahrenheit with one hundred percent humidity. The app said it felt like a hundred and ten—normal for the end of summer. Compared to where they'd just been, it was nice and cool.

The base lay just ahead, adjacent to a hydroelectric dam far from a major population center, and not many people would have recognized it as a base. The perfect location for a unit that didn't exist.

"We're home, boys," Tomlin said.

Jermaine Hyde looked his way and nodded. The man said nothing, but he smiled for a moment. Hyde had a great smile that he almost never used. Some things just weren't meant to be seen by the world at large.

It was almost eight hundred hours. The day was just beginning.

2

•

Woodhurst looked at his reflection and found everything in order. His uniform was crisp, his hair was in place. None of the rest mattered.

However, the latest trip to DC hadn't gone the way he wanted and despite his best efforts he couldn't make his jaw unclench.

When he left his quarters, Pappy was waiting for him.

Roger Elliott wasn't a military man—not any more. He hadn't been for a long time, but Woodhurst got along just fine with him. The man was dressed in black slacks and a black t-shirt. His hair was too long and he hadn't shaved in a few days. Despite that, the two men had enough in common to guarantee they worked together well.

Woodhurst's charge was to locate and, if possible, capture an alien. A creature not born of this planet. He had a special team of men to help with that. The Reapers were among the best-trained men in the world, capable of striking hard and fast. They could go into unknown territory, set up a base of operations, locate and extract their target—all inside of a couple of hours. He knew this for a fact, because they'd been dropped into several different countries and had proven themselves. Computer simulations just confirmed the facts.

As much as he would have loved to take the credit for their skills, Woodhurst wasn't responsible, not really. He oversaw everything, yes, but it was the CIA man who took care of the actual training. Pappy Elliott was old enough that he should seriously consider retirement, but that wasn't likely to happen in this lifetime. Woodhurst could call himself a driven man and mean it. Sometimes he thought Elliott made him look like a slacker.

And Elliott was laser focused on a single objective. More than anything in life, he wanted an alien found, captured, and interrogated or cut apart and studied. He wanted it the way carnivores wanted fresh meat— because unlike everyone else on the Stargazer base, he'd actually *fought* a creature from another planet.

According to the reports, Pappy Elliott had faced an extraterrestrial when he was in Southeast Asia. The details were technically "need to know," but Woodhurst had the need and had studied the files. Whatever Elliott and his men had come up against during the Vietnam War, it had been larger than a man, possessed advanced stealth technology, and it murdered most of his men before vanishing.

There were three very grainy photos of a ship, including one that showed several human bodies in different stages of dismemberment. They'd been "skinned and prepared like deer in hunting season," according to Elliott, and his words were accurate enough. Whatever other evidence might exist, Woodhurst did not know, but the accounts he had heard on many an occasion left him with little doubt.

Elliott remained uncertain as to why he had been allowed to live. It haunted him the way living through a massacre always haunts the survivors. Pappy had been doing covert ops in Vietnam, and despite a small contingent that had shoved aside his claims, Elliott had continued on with the CIA and was still technically a part of the Agency. These days he was on permanent loan to Woodhurst and Project Stargazer.

His obsession over what he had experienced, his desire to know everything there was to know about alien contact, and his skills in wetwork and black ops over the years had guaranteed that he would be an asset.

So far he had never let Woodhurst down.

Elliott nodded when the door opened. Woodhurst nodded back and started walking, and his friend moved into step with him.

"You're not looking happy."

"There's nothing to be happy about," Woodhurst replied.

"Did they cut the budget again?"

Woodhurst snorted. "They cut any further and they're going to find bone."

Elliott nodded. "We need proof."

"It's hard to get proof without some sort of actual encounter, isn't it?" Woodhurst said. "The only physical evidence we've ever had is decades old, and the bean counters have decided it's not 'compelling.' It's been years, and we're still waiting."

"Nothing new since LA."

Woodhurst nodded. It was all he could offer. "Plenty of rumors, but it's the same old song and dance. If there are aliens out there, they're not letting us know, and we need to produce some sort of evidence, or those assholes will find better ways to spend the money."

Elliott made a face. "The evidence they have should be enough."

"Politicians have very short memories, and see what they want to see to further their own agendas," Woodhurst said. "They say it's been decades. All the rumors in the world mean nothing without it." He shrugged. "They've got a point. Twenty-odd years without any new evidence makes it look as if we had a chance encounter, if that. Anything that happened before the official records might as well not exist."

"Maybe we can keep getting extra funding from the Agency. When we loaned out the Reapers, Stargazer got paid for the services rendered."

"That's the only reason they haven't cut us off yet." Woodhurst growled and shook his head. "We're actually proving to be beneficial, but if things don't change soon, they're going to take the Reapers away from us and kill the program."

"Back in the day, when this was the 'Other Worldly Life Forms Program,' the funding was always easy." Elliott shook his head. "Damned politics. I hate this shit."

"We all do. Problem is, these days there are too many

subcommittees and too many watchdog groups. Sliding this sort of project through the microscope and calling it 'research and development' isn't as easy. If we didn't need a special facility and a few transports, it would be easier."

"Fact of the matter is, the Agency *isn't* making it any easier." The other man rolled his shoulders and shook his head. "I mean, it's good when we can deploy the boys and have them help out—that's a nice mark on our side— but it isn't enough, and the guys in charge aren't the same ones any more. No one wants to play nice together."

Woodhurst nodded. "The current administration doesn't like it when people play nicely together. Distraction and confusion are the name of the game. The better to keep your enemies off balance."

That was being kind, and they both knew it. From the Executive branch and through all the varying offshoots, the name of the game was obfuscation. If anyone in the really high echelons had known of the existence of Project Stargazer, they'd have likely moved to shut it down immediately.

Elliott must have been reading his mind again.

"Traeger thinks he has a way around that," he said.

"Yeah? How so?"

"If we can get a little more funding, and maybe make a few small concessions—the sort that don't affect national security, of course—he thinks we could get a lifeline from the private sector."

Woodhurst stopped and stared at the other man.

"Excuse me?"

Elliott held up a hand to ward off his ire.

"Look, I'm not saying I agree with him, I'm just saying it's a consideration," he responded. "If the current administration wants to get into bed with big business and stay there, and we can assume that they do, then the privatization of Stargazer might be the way to go. At least some of it."

Woodhurst frowned.

"We're working with state-of-the-art materials here, Pappy, you know that," he said. "I'm not comfortable with the idea that military technology might get handed out to the rest of the world through some weapons dealers who have the right political clout."

"No one is." Elliott shook his head. "That's not what Will's talking about. He thinks, if we work it the right way, that some of the tech we've got, and anything we discover, could go to medical companies." He sighed. "We're talking an upgrade on how to stitch skin here, not offering new stealth technology to the Chinese."

Woodhurst continued to frown, but he considered the possibilities. New medical technology was an acceptable alternative, in his eyes. There was always room for mending broken bodies. Yet there were other considerations, like data compression. Before OWLF had released some of what they'd uncovered, there hadn't been CDs or DVDs. He didn't understand the technical details, but he'd heard rumors—and only rumors—that the transmissions sent from the aliens had been tagged and identified on long-distance radio signals.

It wasn't until a group at the Massachusetts Institute of Technology had been brought in that they realized how the information was compressed, and discovered methods for mimicking the process. Those were civilians, *students*, without the clearances necessary for such potentially volatile data.

Woodhurst shook his head. No proof. Just rumors. That was part of the reason he didn't much care for the notion of privatizing *any* part of their work. If the wrong tech got to the wrong people, in the wrong countries, it could be mayhem.

"I'm not so sure about that idea, Pappy."

"It's the CDs and DVDs thing again, isn't it?"

"I know, they said they made the discoveries on their own," he answered, "but I still don't like it. What if someone other than us got their hands on a propulsion system taken from a captured vessel? What if someone other than us managed to retrofit a vehicle for space travel?"

"What if Lockheed Martin got a contract to work on military jets with VTOL that were capable of leaving the atmosphere and dropping back into territories over China and Russia? And what if no one else had access to the jets but us?" Elliott shrugged. "It's all just speculation until we get there, but Will might be on to something. I think it's worth considering, if nothing else is going the right way and—let's be honest here, General—nothing's going our way right now."

Woodhurst was still unconvinced.

"Nothing gets past the subcommittees faster than the possibility of a profit," Elliott persisted. "You know it, I know it, and pretty much all of Washington knows it."

Woodhurst nodded, much as he didn't want to. "I'll

think about it." He looked at his friend. "Try to schedule something for Traeger and me if you have a chance, before I head back north."

"Will do," Elliott said. "Been a hot season. Maybe we'll get lucky."

The general knew exactly what he meant. According to the limited research they had in their possession, the aliens seemed to prefer hot weather. He didn't know if it was a necessity based on their physiology, or if they simply preferred the warmer climates, but if his data was accurate, the weather outside was nearly perfect.

"It's one of the hottest summers we've ever experienced, here and everywhere else," he said. "Still, I wouldn't hold my breath. It's not like they're snowbirds, who show up whenever the weather turns."

Elliott shook his head. "No, but I think we're due for a break." That earned him a small snort of laughter and an amused look.

"You send that memo to God for me, will you?"

"You got it."

Woodhurst looked at his watch. "Listen, this is a short break for me. The bean counters decided they need a long weekend, so they sent me home to come up with statistics and keep the song and dance going. We'd better get busy, and I might need you coming with me to DC this time."

Elliott frowned. "Might not be the best time, General. The Reapers just got back from Central America, and it's time for a debriefing." He got a quick smile on his face, and quelled it. "Maybe Traeger can come with you?"

The general nodded. It wasn't a perfect option, but it

might have to do. Traeger was a good bureaucrat, capable, shrewd. That said, Woodhurst had never liked the man very much. He was just a little too slick.

Still, it would be a chance to discuss the notion of outside help.

"He's good at talking people up," Woodhurst admitted. "I just want to make sure he knows what's on the line here, Pappy. You need to make it clear to him."

"As good as done." Elliott looked away from him then, and Woodhurst resisted the urge to nod his head. He knew the problem, of course. Pappy had himself under control. He knew his limits, but there were a few people in Washington who felt relieved to have him away from the Agency, because he had a history.

It was a simple fact—the man had encountered an alien and lived to talk about it, but he had lost a lot of men in the encounter, and had been scarred by it. There were a couple of other survivors who had been just as affected. The difference was, they weren't around.

Woodhurst had never met an alien. He hoped to, at some point, but he wanted it to be under the right conditions. Elliott hadn't been that lucky. The creature he'd described was more than seven feet in height, and physically capable of ripping a man in half. It had killed a dozen people in the middle of a war zone, and it had done the job so spectacularly that the witnesses were never the same afterward.

Good men haunted by what they'd seen, and yet an oversight committee looked at the evidence and saw nothing but numbers. That was the problem Woodhurst was facing. Thinking about it made him want to reach for a few hundred antacids, or maybe a good pistol. Instead he focused on his friend.

"You look stressed, Pappy," he said. "What's happening?"

"Same old, same old." The man turned his way and shrugged. He looked into Woodhurst's eyes. "It's the weather, you know. Affects my nerves. It always makes me antsy." The general nodded, and they started walking again. Deep abiding heat and heavy humidity seemed to be part of the way these things played out, and for Pappy they would always be a reminder.

Every account they'd found, going back for a long stretch of time, said things hunted people in weather like this. Most of them were old rumors, or tales passed down through family lines, but Elliott and others had done a great deal of research into the matter. There were a few reports that were newer, that were—frankly—more concrete. Reports from men in the military, in the CIA, and on the streets of Los Angeles. Solid reports.

Evidence, if not in physical form.

Of course, that was the problem. They needed something solid, something that could be used by the military, for military purposes. Lacking that, they were losing the impetus to keep the cash flowing as was necessary to run the operations.

Even one piece of evidence—one solid, tangible, recognizable object—would make a difference. Yet whatever the things were that came in the hot seasons, and hunted human beings as if they were game on a preserve, they were careful not to leave evidence. Careful enough that in at least one incident they had devastated an area as large as half of Manhattan, just to clean up after themselves.

At least according to the reports.

Just how often do the fuckers come here? Woodhurst wondered.

"Well, we can hope that this time around your nerves get us a blip on the radar," he said with a wry smile. "Anything at all would be better than nothing, if you get my meaning."

"I do." Elliott nodded his head. "I keep hoping."

"We have the team. Now we just need a target." Woodhurst stopped in front of his office door. "Not that I don't appreciate all that you've done, but it would be nice if we could stop loaning our boys out to your bosses. Sooner or later someone might get lucky and put one of them out of commission, and I don't much like that idea."

"Are you going to be there for the debriefing?"

"Yeah. I'll be there. I just need to gather some of my paperwork first. No rest for the wicked." Woodhurst smiled, and this time it was a genuine expression of warmth. He liked Elliott. The man was a solid asset and good company, too. He played a mean game of chess.

"I'll get 'em set up for you, General."

"Much obliged."

3

The sun was up. The clouds obscured the light a bit, but took nothing away from the heat of the day. A dozen different insects buzzed around him, but they were not a concern. As a part of his standard regimen, he'd inoculated himself against any possible microbial infections they might carry.

The trees around him were draped with moss and their bark was damp above the waterline. This was one of those areas where the tides from the ocean changed the levels of the water significantly—that, or the area had a wet season that had just passed.

It hardly mattered.

The day was ripe and full of promise, and he was here for a hunt.

He had traveled a very long way to get here, had planned and prepared for this. There were contingencies and redundancies. There were weapons. There were maps. There were devices for cleaning his prey and preparing them for display.

He had time, as well. He had all that was needed to ensure that this was a successful hunt.

Of course, others had believed that before, and come back disappointed or simply not come back at all. That was the thrill of a good hunt. The best hunts, the ones that mattered, were the ones where there was an element of danger. Hunting prey that could not hunt back was like stalking a plant that could not move or defend itself.

If he wanted to be a farmer, he would grow crops.

He wanted blood. He wanted the thrill of a target that could bare its teeth and strike hard enough to kill. There were creatures on this planet that thrived on bloodshed. How could that not be a thing of beauty?

A few buttons pushed on the wrist gauntlet, and his ship was hidden away.

He was tempted to take off his war mask and breathe the air here. According to his father the atmosphere was thin and tasted of pollutants, because the locals were still not wise enough to care for their own world. There had been a time when the whole planet was cooler. It had been harder to endure the climate then, and find a good hunting spot, but these days it was almost as if the local inhabitants wanted to be targeted, hunted, and killed.

Sometimes the prey made it easy to find them.

In the distance an avian let out a high, loud screech. Closer by, a primitive motor pushed a vessel over the surface of a local waterway.

Behind his war mask he bared his teeth in a battle grin.

The hunt was on.

N N N

The heat was staggering. Neal Foster had grown up in Florida and had lived near the Okefenokee his entire life, but he couldn't remember a time when the heat and the sticky humidity had mixed together so perfectly, to leave every person covered in a layer of sweat.

Next to him on the skiff, Cooper Monroe was scratching at the back of his neck. He moved so violently that the boat actually shifted a bit.

"One more goddamn mosquito bites me," he growled loudly enough to be heard over the motor, "I swear I'm burning everything in sight."

"I told you to put on the repellant. Do you listen to me? No." Foster knew the truth. Coop was happiest when he was bitching.

"I put the shit on my skin," he protested. "Then I sweated it off. Fuckin' rip-off."

Foster chuckled. "Well, maybe you should move back up to North Carolina," he said. "Won't catch any 'gators, but you won't sweat quite as much, either."

"Just as hot there as it is here."

"That's a certified pile of bullshit." If there was a certain sense of pride in Foster's voice when he talked about how miserable it was to live in Florida in this kind of heat, it was only because he'd endured it so many times over the years. The Okefenokee in the summertime held a promise of a special sort of misery, and the mosquitoes were a part of it, of course. The nasty bastards should have been claimed as the state bird, especially in this area. His mom used to joke about the damned things carrying babies away late at night. He figured she wasn't too far off the mark.

"Might not be true," Coop said, "but it's close."

Foster peered out over the water. "We might have to go home—even the 'gators are staying away in this heat."

"What? And waste three hours? We still have beers." Coop was grinning as he spoke. That was one of the things Foster liked about the man. He had the right priorities, and a proper sense of humor. Even bad jokes were funny if you had enough beers in you.

They moved in under the cypress trees, into the shadows that danced on the water. Coop turned his head sharply and he frowned. It wasn't a look of anger or disappointment so much as it was concentration. He had what Foster's mom had laughingly called his "resting psycho face." Whenever he started thinking, he looked like he wanted someone dead.

"What's up?"

"Hang on. I think I saw something." There were cypress trees all around them, and the area was half obscured by the veils of Spanish moss draping across the northern branches of the things. Down and up alike they were heavy, and the stains of algae on the water were clear to the naked eye. Nothing moved in that water—Foster would have seen it.

He looked at Coop and followed his gaze to where the man was staring. There was nothing to see.

"You think it's a cop?" He kept his voice low. Alligators were technically on the endangered list. They weren't exactly supposed to be hunting for the massive reptiles, strictly speaking, and there were ugly fines and jail time to be considered.

"Not unless cops move in the branches."

Foster grinned. "Most of the cops in Coyahunga County couldn't climb a tree if they had to." He wasn't completely wrong. Maybe half could do it, but they'd be pissed off about it. The other half tended to be a bit out of shape. Not obese, exactly, but working in that direction. Southern cooking did that to a man.

"I'm telling you I saw something," Coop replied. "Might be those bastards are using drones to film us."

Well, shit, that was a serious consideration. Photographic evidence and all that. He gestured for Coop to hand him the bag with the shotgun. He wasn't exactly an Olympic-level skeet shooter, if such a beast existed, but he could take down a drone if he had to, and would if they spotted one.

"I don't like that idea, Coop. Not even a little." The shotgun came out and was loaded in a matter of seconds. He could have done the job with his eyes closed.

"Ain't going on my list of top tens any time soon."

"I'm guessing we should head home. This just isn't the right day for 'gators."

"Isn't the right day."

From ten feet away, to the north, he heard the words echoed very clearly. The sound came from above him, and something was *off* about it. Without even thinking about it Foster took aim with the double barrels. He didn't pull the trigger, though—he wasn't stupid, just a little paranoid now that drones were a consideration.

Three points of red light struck his left eye and he squinted against the unexpected glare.

What the hell?

Coop shouted, "Don't move! They've got a laser sight on your head."

"From a goddamned drone?" he said, panic running through him. "What? Is it armed now?" Still, he listened. Better not to take any chances.

Then the light was gone, and a second later three points of red were painting the side of Coop's head.

"Jesus, Cooper. What the fuck is that?"

"Isn't the right day," came the voice again, and Foster looked up.

Something moved above them. The branches of the cypress tree groaned audibly. Whatever it was, he couldn't see it—it must have been camouflaged. There was motion, but his eyes wouldn't focus on anything. The branches and the green and the cloudy blue sky were all there, but distorted, sort of like a bad picture on a computer screen.

Foster adjusted the shotgun a bit. "Whoever's out there, I'm not playing with you," he said loudly.

"Not playing." The words were closer now, and he swung the shotgun around, aiming almost directly above them. Wood creaked and the leaves above his head rustled. There was something on the closest branch of the heavy tree, or maybe just above it. Maybe it *was* a drone, with a loudspeaker. That would explain the weirdness of the voice.

Enough. He had no intention of getting tagged by the cops.

The report from the 12-gauge was like thunder. It was just a warning shot. Several birds took flight at the sound, and at the same time, the shotgun was ripped from Foster's hand, causing him to bellow in pain. He wasn't a weak man, and he'd had a firm grip, but the weapon was wrenched away and his index finger—still tucked in the trigger guard—snapped in half.

Then his chest was torn open as twin metal trenches appeared in Foster's torso, and blood started to spurt out. At first it seemed surreal, and he didn't feel anything, then the pain slammed through him. His limbs stopped working and he fell backward in the skiff. Through dimming eyesight he saw his friend.

Something violent happened to Coop's throat.

4

The general was speaking and they listened. It was the same old business. More preparation, more possibilities of covert ops to keep them ready for when the time came. The old man was stressed. They could all see it, but no one said anything.

"So that's where we stand, gentlemen," Woodhurst said. "I'm heading back to DC again to work out the details of our funding. In the meantime, as always, you keep up your training with Mr. Elliott."

The general did not have to give a sign that he had finished. They knew him well enough, and so as one they rose from their seats.

"Yes, sir!" they said in unison. A moment later Woodhurst was gone, and they settled into their seats again to listen to Elliott. The look on his face was even more telling.

"The general's being nice, he's not saying how bad it is. There's a serious chance of getting our budget cut again, and that means there's a decent likelihood that Stargazer will be eliminated." He stopped to let that sink in.

Traeger didn't say a word. None of them did. They weren't supposed to, and they knew it.

"I got a report or two already from your last visit out of country. All I can say is, good work. That's a nest of snakes that won't bite anyone again." He looked pleased now, then his expression changed. He seemed to be searching for something he wanted to say.

"So, listen, straight shit time. I know what all of you signed on for, and I want that, too—more than you know. I want us to find and capture one of these aliens. I mean that. I've seen one, I've fought one, and I've watched the bastard kill a lot of good men." His expression hardened. "We need to get our hands on one of them just to level the playing field. Forget all the rest of it—we need a win, boys, and I don't mean a win for the Agency.

"You've been doing a damned fine job, and making me look good in the process." Elliott smiled. "But we need the real deal, and there's nothing you or I can do about that. We don't have any secret way of contacting the aliens— picking up our goddamned smartphones and calling them. If we did this would all be easier. I'm just..." He paused a moment, and looked around the room, making eye contact with each member of the team.

"Just make sure you stay ready," he said. "That's all. I have a feeling. It's damned hot out there, and I think sooner rather than later we're going to be hunting one of these bastards down. At least I sure as hell hope so."

Elliott rolled his shoulders and shook his head.

"Go get some rest while you can."

Tomlin nodded and stood up. It was another variation of the same speech they'd had a dozen times before. *"Be prepared, hurry up and wait."* Military speak for "sometime, maybe soon, maybe not." He could see it in the expressions on the rest of the Reapers. They felt the same way—except for Strand, who looked ready to get drunk and wild. He wouldn't go far, but odds were the man would soon be killing a few thousand enemies on a video game while he knocked back a twelve-pack.

It was time for them to blow off steam, and Tomlin decided to let it go. He could have reminded them that *technically* they were always on call, but it wouldn't do anyone any good. He couldn't push too hard when downtime came around.

Pulver, Burke, and King headed for the mess hall, and Tomlin thought that sounded like a mighty fine idea. Chow and coffee were two of his favorite ways to relax, and he could do both while he finished filling out the reports.

Hill would do what Hill always did—a shower and then off to work out. He could hardly be number one if he was idle. Orologas was already chasing after Elliott and hoping that, maybe, somehow, the old man had found another sound bite to play with.

The communications specialist came to a stop when Traeger showed up. The man in the gray pinstriped suit and crisp white shirt held up one hand, and Orologas put on the brakes. Traeger had the clothing and all the right expressions and gestures to come across as a smooth operator. He always had a smile and flawlessly paid attention to whatever it was someone was saying to him. He was courteous and polite, efficient and friendly.

Tomlin trusted him not at all.

Traeger was too smooth, too friendly, and just a little greasy under his six-hundred-dollar suit. Generally he wore fatigues, but not when he was traveling. Smiling a silent thank you to Orologas, he moved over to Elliott with a confident stride.

"Just making sure I got this right, Pappy," he said. "I'm going to DC with the general?"

Elliott nodded his head. "I can't be in two places at once, and last I checked you were the man with the ability to sweet talk an angry mob." He smiled at his own joke. "They may not be angry, but the subcommittee is definitely a mob."

"Just making sure," Traeger responded. "The general said it, but you know I answer to you."

Elliott smiled indulgently. "It's you. We need a push. They're trying to cut us apart, William. I can't go in there and work a group of politicians as well as you can. We should always know our strengths, and we definitely need to know our weaknesses, so if you could do this for me, I'd appreciate it."

Traeger smiled. "Like I need an excuse to get out of this heat?" He let out a small chuckle. "I'll be on the next plane."

"I appreciate you, William." Elliott clapped the younger man on the shoulder and headed for his office. "Never doubt that." As he reached the door, he turned and said, "Remember, though—that place is built on a swamp." Then he disappeared out into the hall. Once in his office, Elliott would sit there and wait patiently until Tomlin delivered his report.

That was one reason Tomlin always tried to be prompt.

When Elliott was sitting alone in his office, there was a chance he would do something foolish. It had only happened twice, but Tomlin was aware that Pappy liked to take a nip now and then to calm his nerves. Nothing major, never enough to cloud his judgment, but that wasn't the point.

He had a reputation among certain people for being a whack-job. He was a damned fine instructor, and he took his work seriously, but just as the people in Washington were having trouble with the idea of aliens, a lot of the folks around Stargazer had trouble with the notion that Elliott was alive when he'd lost an entire team in a combat zone.

No one really said anything, but they didn't need to, either. Anyone who worked in the military long enough learned how to read faces. It was the side glances and small expressions that people made when Pappy walked past that told Tomlin what he needed to know.

Despite his desire to take Tomlin's place, more than once Hill had expressed concern over those looks. To Tomlin's knowledge Hill had never caught that whiff of alcohol on the man's breath. He wondered how Hill would react if he did.

Alcoholism was a bad thing. It might be a disease, according to a lot of people, but there was no place in the military for men too weak to control their baser urges. At least not if the men were in charge. It was a weakness in the eyes of most, and Elliott suffered from that weakness.

Tomlin intended to make sure it didn't bite the man too hard, at least not before the Stargazer group was set up to last.

It was a situation that needed watching. To that end Tomlin hustled himself to the commissary with his iPad and got down to the business of eating and writing reports.

N N N

Elliott didn't need to write any reports. He'd already handled that before he sent the Reapers into action. The plan was direct and when it was all said and done, the Reapers had done their job.

He would forward the paperwork from Tomlin and Hill, and add a note if he needed to, but probably he wouldn't waste his time. The boys knew what they were doing. If he'd had any part in teaching them the importance of their work, so much the better.

His hands were shaking. He hated that more than he could ever express. It didn't happen every damned time the weather pushed over a hundred degrees Fahrenheit, but it happened often enough. Roger Elliott was a man who was haunted by his past. He knew it, and so did the people above him, but there were benefits that compensated for the risks of his situation.

For one thing, he was the only man they could convince to work with them who had ever run across one of the hunting aliens and lived to tell about it. That alone had made him indispensable—up to now.

Elliott sat down on his bed and considered that while he grabbed a smoke. It was a damned stupid habit, and he'd given up cigarettes a dozen times, but now and then he'd get a bad case of the shakes and it was tobacco or booze. The demon alcohol was harder to break free from, so the cigarettes won again.

He felt himself wheeze as he took in the smoke, but held it just the same and let the nicotine soothe away the worst of his frayed nerves. The head rush was enough to make him want to close his eyes and sleep, but that wasn't an option. Instead he lay back and he remembered the reason he was here.

Hanoi had been enlightening.

Saigon was exhilarating and terrifying in equal measures. People got dead over there. People got changed over there.

Roger Elliott got changed.

N N N

How long had they been in the jungle? He couldn't begin to say. All he knew was that the Viet Cong were getting closer and it was his job, along with a small handful of others, to make sure their friends in the south repelled the bastards.

To that end they were training a select handful of Vietnamese in the fine art of terrorist explosives, and educating the same lot on propaganda and psyche techniques. It was grisly work, but somebody had to do it.

Everything was moving along just fine until the first body was found hanging in the trees, skinned alive. It took them far too long to decide if the victim was American or a native. In any event, the locals bugged out so fast they practically left afterimages lingering in the air.

There was no warning. The men they were dealing with simply disappeared. If they hadn't taken their supplies with them, Elliott would have thought the Viet Cong had developed a disintegration ray like in the old films he used to watch at the drive-in.

Carter looked his way and shook his head. Terrence Carter was in charge of the radio contact. He knew all the latest codes and could decipher them without even trying. Elliott told his radio man to communicate with the general in Saigon. The message was coded, of course. It was simple enough, really. When the locals bugged out, that frequently was considered reason enough for the local spooks to fade away.

Not this time. The man in charge wanted them staying exactly where they were, regardless of a skinning. That was hardly the worst thing they'd run across, in any event.

N N N

The second night it was two of the Company's boys that vanished. There were twelve of them left, so the response was immediate. Roger stayed where he was and coordinated along with Carter. Costanza took half the team into the jungle to look around and see what could be seen. Maple took the other half and actively went looking for bodies.

Costanza found nothing. He reported in regularly, but the jungle was keeping its secrets. No Viet Cong, no locals to be seen. They ran across an entire village that had been cleared of people. A dozen huts emptied of their occupants. The only thing left in the area was a goat that had been clearly left out as an offering.

Maple had better luck, depending on the definition of luck. His team ran across a collection of bodies that had been eviscerated. When he called in his voice was hitching and he was deeply unsettled. As a rule Maple did not get nervous, but his voice shook and he had to be cautioned more than once to remember the code they were supposed to be using.

"We found ten people," he reported. "Maybe. It's hard to say. They're all dead, and they didn't die easy. I think most of them were alive when they got torn apart."

Carter shook his head. "Torn apart how?"

"Two of them were skinned. At least three bodies without heads. There are fucking bodies here without spines. You understand me? Something tore their spines out. Broke the ribs away and tore the spinal columns free from the bodies. I don't know what the fuck they're doing, but these guys are animals. I've never seen anyone taken apart this way."

✳ ✳ ✳

Lying in his bunk, Elliott thought about the pictures they'd taken that day—the ones that Maple had brought back and developed for him to see.

Remembering, he still got the shakes.

✳ ✳ ✳

His bags were packed in short order, and Traeger took them with him to the transport. The general was already there, waiting with that same stoic look that marked most of their encounters.

Woodhurst wasn't a big man, but he carried himself like he was ten feet tall, and he was intimidating at the best of times. The general didn't much like Traeger, he knew, and he was okay with that. Being liked had never been as important as being respected, and Traeger wouldn't have been along for the ride if he didn't have the man's respect. It was that simple.

"Is there a plan in place yet, General?"

"Aside from offering the facts and doing what we can to smooth over the rough patches in the budget, not really." He paused and looked at Traeger carefully, assessing him. "Once we're in the air, I want to hear about your thoughts on outside help."

Traeger nodded his head and offered a smile. That was about what he'd expected. There was a reason he was along for the ride, and it had to do with his connections in all the right places.

He took no particular credit for what had been done, but Traeger was why the Reapers were doing special ops work. It was his idea and his connections that enabled that to happen—with the general's blessing, of course. He didn't take credit because he didn't have to take credit. Everyone who mattered already knew.

Traeger did what had to be done in order to make sure everything worked. It was the way his mother had raised him. It was the way the world had shaped him. Get the job done and make sure every angle was covered. And if possible, make sure you were riding the crest of the wave that resulted, instead of being dragged along in the undertow.

The general was looking out the closest window, though they hadn't yet even begun to taxi. Traeger knew the score. Given a chance to socialize, the general would find someone else to chat with. That was okay, too. Traeger had work to do.

"I can't remember who is on the committee," Traeger said. "Who the problem people are. Can you remind me?"

"The big one is Raferty." Woodhurst sighed. "The man wants to put all of his cards into tax cuts. He thinks we're a burden that could be removed."

Traeger laughed. "We aren't even a blip on the radar."

"You know that, I know that. Raferty sees it differently." Woodhurst actually looked toward him, growing animated. "That's what we're up against."

"So, I think I might know who can help us with Raferty," Traeger said, trying not to sound smug. He knew exactly who could help with the senator. The man had his weaknesses, and he'd been caught more than once with women who weren't his wife, in situations that were dubious at best.

"Really?" The general looked at him with new interest.

"Well, it's a little-known secret, but sometimes we in the CIA find out stuff and keep it to ourselves, for just such emergencies." He flashed Woodhurst a smile. "I might be able to work out a conversation with the man."

The general nodded, smiled, and leaned back in his seat. It was a very small smile, and it was there and gone quickly. A step in the right direction then; a small victory. That was all he needed for now.

He'd worry about bigger victories after they took off.

The general had needs. Traeger intended to help him see those needs satisfied. In the process, he would forward his own agenda as much as he could, because that was the way the world worked. A man did what he had to do, so long as he could face himself in the mirror the next day.

Traeger always liked what he saw in the mirror.

5

Devon Hill climbed out of the shower and dried himself quickly, his body shaking from the workout but his mind clearer for the effort.

No one was saying it, but Project Stargazer was on the ropes. Oh, they were talking about budgets, but they always talked about budgets. This was different though. The words were the same, but the body language was a silent scream of panic.

The Reapers? They were just fine. Tomlin was sweating it—he was worried about the chance to fight aliens. Hill wanted it too, but he didn't need it, not the same way that Tomlin did.

He sighed. "There's a reason he's in charge." He dressed quickly, in black fatigues, which was damn near the unofficial uniform of the Reapers. Then he moved to his desk. Tomlin had filled out the reports. When he was done, Hill looked them over and took notes, then filed them. *You want to know your enemy? You have to study him.*

Tomlin wasn't an enemy, not really, but he was competition. Hill admired Tomlin too much to ever consider him anything less than an associate, and most days he could even call the man a friend. He would certainly follow his orders without hesitation, because the man knew his business.

No, it wasn't that Tomlin wasn't good, it was that Hill needed to be better. No one seemed to want to understand that part, and it wasn't a black-or-white thing, either, though maybe that had some small part in the equation. No, it was simply that his mother had taught him to be the best he could be in all things.

"You gonna do a job?" she said to him. "Make sure no one does it better. You gonna run a hundred-yard dash? Be faster. Work harder for it. Make sure that everyone knows who the winner is, even before you hit the finish line."

"Why?"

"Because no one remembers the guy who came in second."

Just that simple.

Hill shook his head. Second place would do if it was all you could manage, but he had plans that went beyond that. He had no intention of sabotaging anyone. He knew a few who would, like Traeger, the ghost that ran around playing second fiddle to Pappy. Traeger was exactly the sort that liked to take each person's measure to see who he could turn with a few words and a smile.

Traeger wasn't trustworthy. It was *exactly* that simple. He had the right idea—he wanted to win—but he had no sense of honor.

No. Hill intended to do his absolute best as second in

command to Tomlin. He just also intended to be prepared, if anything should happen to the man that meant he had to be replaced. That was the way it worked, in the military and in the real world.

He scanned every line of Tomlin's reports and examined them as carefully as he would study battle plans. The devil was in the details. He just had to figure out which details kept Old Scratch well hidden.

He'd figure it out eventually.

In the meantime, he had plenty to take care of. Orologas was busy with his pet project, trying to understand an alien voice—if that's what it was. Strand was busy trying to find a way to be an even better marksman. Back in his college days the man had won a bunch of awards for marksmanship and quick-draw maneuvers. These days he was too busy worrying about whether or not someone would take away his rights as a gun enthusiast. There was no chance of that, but he remained convinced that his rights were at stake every single time a shooter went nuts somewhere in the US, which seemed to happen at least once a week of late.

Pulver and Hyde were easy. They loved their work. If they had a care in the world beyond what they did for a living, they hid it well enough to fool anyone looking, and he made it a habit to look. Why? Because the job of the commanding officer was to command, and the job of his second was to make sure everything ran smoothly.

King wanted world peace. He also wanted proof there was life on other planets. Hill wasn't sure exactly what had happened to King in the past, but the man wanted to know about aliens the same way that some holy rollers wanted to know about God Almighty. King didn't seem to care much what sort of aliens there were. It was more like the man was on a personal quest to prove something, if only to himself. He was a quiet fanatic.

For King to be truly happy, there had to be some form of life beyond the Earth. There had to be, or what was all the fuss about? He claimed to be an atheist, but Hill suspected he was just looking for the right religion.

Did that mean King would hesitate when the time came?

No. Hill didn't think so. If he believed otherwise he would have brought the matter to Tomlin's attention, and to Elliott's as well. King didn't pose a risk to the team, nor did any other member. Not even Strand, though Burke worried about him from time to time. He had all the signs of a loose cannon, at least on the surface. Hill and Burke had discussed the man on several occasions, and as far as they could tell, despite his wild side, the man was loyal and did his job without reproach. He just needed to vent when he was done, and as long as that happened on the base, there was no harm.

And if it happened off base?

Well, then Hill would make sure he was there to handle the situation, or Burke would be there for the same reason. All in a day's work.

Hill leaned back at his small desk and contemplated the files he'd read. There were no inaccuracies to notice. He'd looked for them actively, and found none. That was a-okay. Devon Hill was nothing if not patient. In the meantime, it might be time for a few rounds with a punching bag, or possibly with a living opponent if he found one in the area.

There was always time for training. Razor edges didn't just happen.

They had to be sharpened and honed.

6

Biker Week was coming soon, and that meant it was time to get the motorcycles overhauled and tuned.

That responsibility fell to Andy Simon and he took it seriously. The local chapter of the Four Horsemen were the best of the best, and they were going to look like it, especially since they were hosting the event. Simon was a mechanic and he was one of the best in the area. His membership in the Horsemen was strictly honorary, since he did not ride a bike and couldn't if his life depended on it. A wreck a few years back had ended his days of riding with the others.

Despite many attempts to remember what had happened, Andy couldn't have said exactly how he managed to get wedged between a tractor trailer and an SUV. He could just tell you that the end result was a pair of legs that didn't work and a bike that had been scattered over a fifth of a mile along I-85.

He was alive, and that counted. None of the guys made

fun of him, or if they did, they were smart enough to do it where he couldn't hear it and where the man in charge of the charter, Burly Hanscomb, couldn't hear it either. Before the accident they'd been as close as brothers. Now it wasn't quite the same, but Burly had a loyal streak half a mile long and no one got to mess with Andy and keep walking.

To repay the loyalty Andy ran the garage for the club and he did it with pride. He made sure the bikes were in perfect order and spent a lot of time detailing them with the sorts of illustrations that would have cost a fortune for anyone who wasn't a member. A knack for art and a top-of-the-line airbrush setup meant the boys were always glad to see him.

Hell, they'd even put in a ramp to make sure he could get into the clubhouse with ease. Maybe not the best choice, considering what Stew had done with his Harley when he was a bit too drunk, but the door got fixed and Stew promised never to do it again, so there was that to consider.

Tom-Tom Willis was sitting at the edge of Andy's desk, his heavy posterior resting on a grease stain, and smoking one of his obnoxious cigars. His hair was tied back in a ponytail and his five o'clock shadow had progressed to the beginning of a beard. He was eyeing the work on his hog with the eye of a connoisseur, not that he would have known art from a postage stamp.

"What do you think?" Andy asked, though he suspected he already knew the answer.

Willis squinted for a moment and then sighed happily.

"Looks good as new, brother!"

Andy nodded and grinned. "Well, the scratches were

bad, but not enough to ruin the original work. I just sort of traced it." That was a lie. He'd had to do some serious repairs, but he didn't mind—Tom-Tom was one of the good ones.

"Nah!" Willis shook his head. "I saw the damage. You can't even see the scratches any more. That's awesome."

Not far away the sounds of partying issued from the clubhouse. Andy figured to get himself over there just as soon as he could, but business first.

"How much do I owe you?" Willis's voice stayed cheerful. His eyes grew shrewd.

"Call it two hundred?" Andy threw a low number. He hated haggling.

Tom-Tom smiled. A second later the first scream came from the clubhouse. It was a raw, primal sound, a bellow of pain, and both of them looked through the glare of the midday sun with matching expressions of surprise.

"Better not be anyone causing shit today." Willis shook his head and started for the club. All of the pleasant faded from his demeanor as he walked, and the man moved fast, looking like nothing so much as a lumbering bear on the prowl.

The second scream came from a different throat. Andy couldn't have said who it was, but he knew the voice just the same. There was a .45 in his work bag, and he grabbed it as he started toward the clubhouse. The gun stayed in his lap, his hands pushing the wheelchair hard, following after his friend.

Tom-Tom was through the door and had it closed before he got there and maybe, just maybe, that was a blessing. He couldn't see the fight but he heard it. It sounded like Billy was screaming something, but his words were too distorted to make out. Billy, who liked to talk about his time as a mixed martial arts tournament fighter, short-lived though it was. Billy, who bragged about his years of training.

Billy, who came crashing through the window not far from the door, his face torn into shreds and his entire body twitching as he landed on the walkway and flopped around for a moment, like a fish out of water.

"Bill? What the fuck!"

"Ruh, Anny." He was choking on blood. *"Ruhhn."*

It took Simon a moment. The words didn't make sense at first. He had to think about it before *"Run, Andy. Run"* made any sense.

Before Billy could say anything else something smashed into the wall and the entire house shook from the impact, glass fragments falling from the window. Rather than wait for an invitation, Andy rolled forward and pushed at the door. It didn't budge at first, but after a second he managed to wrangle the door open, cursing his useless legs as he often did.

The chaos inside was more than anything he could have expected. As he pushed the door open his eyes adjusted to the gloom, and he saw more and more of the inside of the clubhouse. The pool table was knocked on its side, two of the legs broken away. One of the guys—it looked like Harry—was draped over it in a position that wasn't natural. His back was bent too far for him to be alive, or at least functioning. He remembered when his own spine had bent that way.

theorized that the species genome was being altered to improve the species as a whole.

No. He could not continue down that path. This was his time away, his time to prove his value in a more traditional sense. This was the time to hunt.

The winds picked up enough to make him adjust his stance. Down below him two of the creatures staggered, caught off guard by the violent blast of air. Several humans looked around, and at least one made a high-pitched barking sound that might have indicated amusement, but seemed devoid of humor.

Enough. He was done hunting for the night and had other things to consider. The temperature was perfect, but so far the pursuit, the combat, had been too easy. He would seek a more challenging target. His chieftain had said once that at times patience was required. The locals would see their fellow creatures fall and call in hunters better equipped to fight a true threat.

He had left a great enough trail of destruction. If that was the case on this planet, they would come for him soon enough. When they did, he would be ready for a worthy hunt.

7

The rain misted across the runway when they landed in DC. Woodhurst climbed from the plane and crossed the tarmac without any ceremony, or even an umbrella. Traeger wasn't quite as fast about it. There was an overcoat to put on. It was hardly a serious storm, but he hated getting wet when he was dressed for business.

The jeep that picked them up had a top. Good enough. Woodhurst said nothing, but stared out the window, his face set in a brooding look of concentration. Traeger pulled out his phone and started sending text messages. There were several favors he needed to call in if things were going to go the way he wanted, and now was as good a time as any to start the balls in motion.

Phil Amsburg was the personal aide of Senator Laurel, who was on the committee that overlooked Stargazer. Amsburg was available for drinks at 3:00 PM at the Madison Hotel. That worked for Traeger. He had nothing on the senator, but he knew Amsburg would be able to at least get the woman to consider listening to a few suggestions—because he had plenty on Amsburg. Enough to see the man jailed. Not that he would, of course. A man in prison was nowhere near as useful as a man on the sidelines of the senate.

Four more quick text messages guaranteed that he'd be busy for the next day or so, and that was good. As soon as Woodhurst had brought him up to speed, he had begun considering how to work on the problems facing Project Stargazer.

Senator Raferty would be the most problematic, but that was okay for the moment. He had enough to keep him from growing bored while he worked out all the details. A plan of attack was beginning to take shape, and if everything went the way he knew it would, the general was going to consider him a very important man in the very near future.

* * *

Jerry Entwhistle stared at the computer on his desk and yawned. It was late and there was remarkably little to do. His job was to watch the news feeds for anything that might lead them to the Stargazer quarry.

The software was impressively well designed—the parameters were solid and he'd lost count of the number of flags they employed. Just an hour earlier he'd thought he had something when a report came in concerning a series of violent deaths in Montana, but they found the perfectly human sicko who'd been carving parts off of people.

Since then, nothing. Seemingly endless reports of violence, but nothing that would indicate extraterrestrials.

Then that changed.

The report was simple enough, and as he read it he quickly spotted the indicators. There were several survivors—three women and two men—who gave a lot of details. The rest of the folks who'd been attacked were dead, and trophies had been taken. That was a serious red flag. Skin, two skulls and a spine that was removed with unsettling brutality.

The clincher was a phosphorescent substance that could not be identified. One of the people said it came from a ghost he shot.

Bingo.

Jerry got on the phone and called Agent Elliott. The older man picked up immediately.

"Pappy. Go."

"Hey, Pappy," Entwhistle said, holding the phone between his ear and shoulder. "I think we may have a sighting for your primary target."

There was a brief pause, the sound of shuffling, and he could imagine the older man grabbing a pen and paper.

"Where?"

"Deer Water Springs, Florida."

"When?"

"Earlier today. There was a biker gang that got themselves, well, killed off. Dismembered, like you said."

"Is this a rumor, or an official report?"

"Official," Entwhistle confirmed. "Just came in."

Elliott paused again. "Send it to me, Jerry."

Still holding the phone, Entwhistle started typing furiously, excitement rippling through him.

This could be it! He waited until he'd finished emailing the file via the secure server, and then said, "Should be yours, sir."

"If this is real, I owe you a beer, Jerry," Elliott said. "Hell, I'll buy a round for the whole crew. Thanks very much." He cut the connection, and Entwhistle nodded to himself, letting out a nervous whistle. Agent Elliott was a nice enough guy, but he'd heard stories about how he was when he was angry. Jerry never wanted to find out personally.

The phone still by his ear, he tapped in the number for the second name on his list.

"Woodhurst." He was on speakerphone.

He gave the general the same report he'd given to Elliott. The officer was cordial and polite and thanked him. Agent Traeger, who was second to Agent Elliott, was there as well. The guy thanked him profusely, and then asked for a follow-up as soon as he knew anything. Traeger was as friendly as anyone he knew and so he was glad to help.

One more call to make. Tomlin. By the time he'd finished, the Reapers were getting ready for departure. They'd need details. It only took a moment to find the town of Deer Water Springs on the map. It was a small place, surprisingly close to the Georgia-Florida line.

They'd be there in no time.

ⵜ ⵜ ⵜ

Pappy Elliott looked on and said nothing as the men he'd trained prepared themselves for a combat situation. There was nothing he needed to say, nothing he *could* say that hadn't been said countless times before.

He'd described in great detail the events in Vietnam that had led him to be their primary instructor. It was simple really—he was the only man available who'd fought one of the nightmares and lived to tell the tale. Well, the only one who was willing to talk about it, at least. He'd met the others. Elliott had been there each time they'd debriefed the few people they could find who'd encountered one of the creatures from another planet.

None of them ever walked away from the encounter unchanged. Death did that. He'd seen plenty of death in his time, but little of it had come from somewhere else, and most of it had at least seemed to make sense. Not the killings by these... these predators. Their motives remained a mystery.

He knew more than most and more importantly, he was willing to share his knowledge. Still, there was only so much he could tell them, and so many ways he could spin it. So he watched his team in silence and thought back to the nightmare he'd faced in the jungles of Southeast Asia.

Seven feet tall if it was an inch. They'd shot out the protective lens over one eye, and beneath it was a visage that had haunted him for decades. A dozen different renderings had been made based on his descriptions and from the other accounts, and he had copied all of them in his personal files. The one thing the renderings had in common, aside from a remarkable level of accuracy, was that they paled in comparison to the real monster.

The soldiers he'd trained—still barely men in his eyes, since he had a lot of years on them—were likely to face a creature he didn't think anyone could be prepared to encounter. It was larger than any of them, stronger by far, and capable of hiding in plain sight. Still, he had trained the Reapers as best he could. They had the best equipment that money could buy—portable, lightweight, and lethal.

They were capable fighters, each among the most competent soldiers that had ever existed. He knew it because he had trained them and found others who could train them well, in a variety of disciplines. Along the way each of the men had lasted through battles that would have left most soldiers dead, and they'd done so without losing a single member of the unit.

Even so, he was worried. The otherworldly life form was deadly on levels they had never encountered. It likely carried tech they could only imagine. However, in the last forty or so years American military technology had expanded by leaps and bounds. The equipment he'd used against the creature would be considered antique in this day and age.

Yet the alien possessed the ability to travel between worlds. Its own science would have advanced over the years. They were nowhere near the weapons the thing would carry.

Pappy hoped he was wrong.

Most likely he wasn't. He remembered.

∕ ∕ ∕

Back in Vietnam, things had been relatively calm in the camp. The usual security, and it was likely the Viet Cong didn't yet know they were there. Then Maple showed him the pictures they'd taken of the remains, and they went on high alert. The enemy was near, and vicious beyond what they'd expected.

The general wanted to know what the blue hell was going on in those woods. Given the sheer savagery of the murders, they pumped up security and slept in shifts—four hours on and four hours off. Half of them guarded the perimeter. The other half, the ones who drew the short straws, went out into the jungle and searched.

For two days and nights all was quiet. Elliott began thinking that they'd lucked out, and that whoever was doing the killings had made their point and moved on. It was, frankly, exactly the sort of thing they taught their allies to do, only taken to a much darker extreme. Hell, as unsettled as he was by the tactic, he could see the benefits of increasing the violence factor so radically.

Then on the third morning Costanza, Gorman, and Harris didn't come back from their patrol of the area. There was no radio contact. There were no flares. Nothing. Everyone in the camp was unnerved.

That night they were found, and Elliott saw the savagery firsthand. All three heads were gone. Their weapons were there—the enemy hadn't bothered to take them. One of them hadn't even been fired. A huge tree had been blown apart and several thick shards of wood were buried in Harris's arm. A land mine? Doubtful, since the explosive pattern didn't match.

Then what had it been?

The next report to the general resulted in a furious

demand for action. So the next day, all of the remaining agents went hunting. They did it together, thinking there would be safety in numbers.

N N N

Remembering made Pappy desperate for a drink.

8

Adrenaline wanted to dance through his body, but Tomlin did his best to suppress that overpowering nervousness. Next to him Hill was already suited up and double-checking his supplies. The man looked in his direction and, despite his usual demeanor, he smiled.

"Gonna be a damned fine day, I can feel it."

Tomlin smiled back. "I think you're right, but let's not get too cocky. These things are supposed to be as tough as they come."

"We can only hope." Hill's smile didn't fade in the least. "We've got this. Been practicing long enough. We've got the best equipment. We've got the best trained. Let's do it."

Tomlin smiled. The enthusiasm, especially from Hill, was contagious.

"Hoo… rah."

"Damn right."

They moved quickly, each member of the team heading

to their assigned location on the transport helicopter. The bird was designed with stealth in mind, and while it had the necessary equipment, it didn't have call signs—or any identifying marks. The bird, much like the occupants, was designed for anonymity.

Tomlin gave the pilot the go-ahead, and a moment later they were airborne, moving into the dark sky.

"What's the situation, chief?" Pulver's voice was tense. He didn't like surprises. None of them did, really, but for Pulver the call to leave his bed was practically a declaration of war. There wasn't much he liked better than a decent night's sleep.

"Looks like we might finally get what we've been after," Tomlin said over the comm. "Got a call on what seems to be an actual alien hunter." He peered from one soldier to the next as he spoke. "If that's the case, we're going hunting for something that stalks and kills our species. God knows why. Near as anyone can tell, there's one or more of these things in a town just south of the Georgia line."

As with Hill before them, the men grinned at the idea. Well, most of them. Hyde didn't smile—he was already in what Orologas had once jokingly referred to as "kill mode." Once a mission started, there was nothing about the man that said he had a sense of humor. Truth be told, that might come in handy.

"We are going into an unknown situation," he continued. "All we have is hearsay so far. What we *do* know is that more than five men were killed by something that, according to the eyewitnesses, could not be seen. Whatever it was it lifted a man who weighed in at over two hundred and seventy-five pounds clean off the ground and gutted him while he was still alive. Whatever it was is supposed to have bled green blood, and left several people alive." He paused. "All of the witnesses were either female or handicapped."

Pulver nodded, understanding immediately.

"Killed all the fighters."

"Exactly. Whatever it was, it only seemed to be interested in skilled combatants. That fits the pattern, and it means that we are officially fucked, gentlemen. We get it, or it gets us." As he said those words, Tomlin smiled. The profile matched what little they knew of the aliens that had hunted people down in Los Angeles, and also along with what little could be gleaned from a dozen other personal accounts.

None of the men looked scared. That was good. He needed hunters on his side, not prey.

"Equipment check. Get it done." The group very quickly went through the collection of high-tech toys they'd been given to handle this task. Tomlin slipped on his night-vision goggles and checked the spectrum of filters. Low light worked, infrared worked, ultraviolet worked. All was well. The radio worked. The rest were in good order. There were, in short, no technical difficulties to get in the way.

"Where are we going to find this thing?" Orologas had finished inspecting his equipment and was putting everything back where it belonged.

"Deer Water Creek, Florida." It was Hill who answered. "A substantial distance from any major urban center."

"Good." Orologas nodded his head and smiled. None of them wanted complications, which was code for none of them wanted witnesses. The fewer people the better for everyone involved.

Pulver shrugged. "Weather's gonna be for shit."

"That may be why we've got this chance at all," Tomlin said. "Worry about what we can control. The rest of it is just the luck of the draw." Pulver offered a very small smile and nodded his head. He knew the drill well enough and was just making conversation.

"Soon enough, gentlemen. We're almost there. When we arrive we monitor the emergency channels and we try to find out what else has gone on."

Hill nodded and added, "These things—we all know this—these things have a pattern. They hunt for a while and they leave. If we're lucky it's just getting started, and we'll have a few chances to find out where it is while it's still on the prowl."

Hyde spoke up, which was a bit surprising. "Are we gonna have access to the police reports?"

Orologas nodded. "I'll have copies of everything they've put on computer as soon as we're settled."

Tomlin closed his eyes as the winds knocked their transport around a little. His body wanted to be active, wanted to be on the move and searching for their hunter from another world. It might be hours, it might be days, but in the meantime all he could do was answer their questions and try to be patient.

N N N

Politics. It was one of the ugliest words ever created, as far as Woodhurst was concerned. The thing about being a soldier was that you wanted the world to be as black and white as possible. When it came to the world of politics, there was no black or white, there was only a spectrum of gray.

There was no battlefront here either. It was just a collection of meetings that had to be played out like a game of chess. Move forward, move to the side, go for the occasional diagonal strike and hope that somehow you got more done than your opponents in the same number of moves.

Except it was more like playing chess with multiple boards and opponents, all coming at you simultaneously. Since he'd arrived in Washington he'd had four meetings with different people, all of whom, on the periphery, could be of assistance.

At that moment a pompous jackass was trying to explain how to make his proposal "sexier," as if the notion of spending millions of dollars to capture an alien stalker and steal its technology should somehow be associated with a pinup in an old *Playboy* magazine. Said jackass, a congressional aide named Norman Mueller, spoke past a mouthful of lamb chop.

"Thing is, unless you can spin this into something that can garner votes, the congresswoman might not be interested in doing anything with it."

"Well, then," the general said, and he smiled, "you might be able to see my problem here. This is strictly need-to-know information, and can't be advertised to the public." It was like trying to explain a circle to someone who had only ever worked with straight lines. "We can't let this get out, because there would be panic."

"What makes you say that?"

"There's no irrefutable proof of life on other planets. If that proof existed, there's every reason to believe that most of the religious groups in this country would go ballistic."

"Why?"

He smiled and considered what it would be like to shove his knife through the damned fool's eye.

"Let's look at the Bible as a good example," Woodhurst said. "Do you see any mention of aliens anywhere in that good book?"

"I'm actually Jewish."

"Fair enough. Are there any mentions of aliens coming down from the stars in the Torah?"

A frown appeared on that bland face. Then, finally, the man shook his head.

"No, not that I can recall."

"So, if I go out there and tell the world that there are aliens, and that they've visited the planet before, and gone hunting people, what do you suppose the response would be from the more devout members of your faith?"

Mueller frowned and thought for a long moment. "Outrage."

Then he added, "Fear."

"Exactly. It's not my place to tell anyone about what's going on here. I'm just a man doing a job. That sort of decision is above my pay scale, and I'm sure the congresswoman would agree with me on that." He shrugged. "My job is simply to get financing so that if and when these things come back, we can try to capture one and see what we can learn from it, including how to stop them from hunting citizens of these United States."

That left the man pondering his position. In the interim, Woodhurst cut a piece of filet from his main course and chewed carefully.

"So there can be no publicity?"

Woodhurst nodded.

"Then I don't know that the congresswoman can help you."

"She's on the committee overlooking my department. She's already working on the situation."

"Well, yes, but can you think of any good reasons for her to support your side of this, over the need to save money?"

"National security."

"We have a council for that, don't we?"

The knife to the eye was sounding better by the second.

Traeger smiled. The meetings continued, but with a twist. There was now a very real hope that the Reapers were onto something.

"Listen, I can't say anything about the situation, except that there's a real chance of, well… instant gratification."

Wayne Raferty stirred the snifter of brandy in his hand and looked at Traeger, feigning boredom. He wasn't bored, Traeger knew, not in the least, but he did his best to fake it because he knew they had something good for him.

"What *can* you tell me?" Raferty said.

"I can tell you that I have interested parties who would provide a lot of the necessary monies for keeping the project afloat, in exchange for a share of the profits down the line."

"Intriguing," the senator responded, "especially since the last I heard this was strictly a need-to-know situation." The man's bushy gray eyebrows moved when he spoke in a way that bordered on distracting.

Traeger nodded. "It *is* need-to-know. I haven't been able to say much to anyone, but it's easy to imagine the opportunities here, for technological advances down the line and the patents they could lead to. The sort of things that make a lot of companies happy to take a risk, even in a situation where they aren't allowed to hear all the details. You get what I'm saying?"

"I do," Raferty said. "Can you tell me which companies are interested?"

"Funny you should ask, Senator. I found a surprising number of companies that would be interested, and that also happen to be part of your stock portfolio." He smiled.

"And how would you know what's in my portfolio, William?" There was a slight edge to the man's voice. It was fully justified.

"You know who I work for. What makes you think I couldn't find out just by asking the right coworker?" Traeger smiled to take the sting out of his words. No one liked knowing their information was more public than they expected, and that definitely included the occasional senator. "Doesn't matter, really. I could have found out by looking into your public records. I might have called in a few favors though. Either way, you have stock in companies that are on my list."

"And do you think that knowledge is going to sway my decision?"

"That's for you to decide, but yes, as a matter of fact, I do." Traeger didn't hesitate in his response. "Look, it comes down to this—no one wants to foot the bill for a project this risky, but it needs to happen, and if a small committee can't make the decision to cover the expenses, we have no choice but to look elsewhere."

The eyebrows met above the man's dark eyes. His expression bordered on contrary, and that wasn't what Traeger wanted at all.

"Where do I come into this?"

Traeger smiled as innocuously as he could manage. "I can't make this happen without support. I can't arrange private funding of a project like this without official backing from a few of the people in the committee. I mean, I probably could—I might manage to hide the paperwork well enough—but if anyone were to ask, I'd be working twice as hard just to hide the information."

Raferty took a very small sip of his brandy and considered the words in silence.

Traeger sighed. The man was playing hard to get.

"It's easy to see why various companies would be interested in this sort of research and development," he said. "Very little risk up front, relatively speaking, and possible rewards that could last for decades. It's a win-win. I get my funding, you get a nice bump in your 401K when things go the way we both know they will."

"You believe things are going to happen?"

Traeger leaned forward, his eyes locked with the senator's. "I believe that right now there's a group of eager soldiers who are doing their best to make this concept a reality. Right now. This. Very. Minute." He tapped the table in front of him. "If we work this the right way, everyone is going to be happy—*very* happy—before the week is through."

The senator said nothing, but he was thinking. That was all Traeger could hope for.

"It costs nothing, Senator," he persisted. "The private sector—select members of the private sector—are willing to take up a lot of the risks. We could stay exactly where we are with government contributions. Hell, maybe if we have to we could even shave away a bit."

The man nodded his head and set down his brandy.

"Best of all," Traeger concluded, "nothing really changes, and no one is the wiser." Done with his part of the sales pitch, he picked up his own snifter and swished the brandy around in his hand, warming the fluid before taking a very small sip.

Victory came in small doses, much like brandy. And just as with the liquor, it was meant to be savored.

9

The rains came down harder still, assaulting the ground with hard droplets that splashed back up in retaliation. The air was thick with the downpour, which nearly eliminated any chance to see beyond a few feet.

The slashing wind took that torrential rain and turned it sideways. Cars rocked where they rested or, if they were moving, hydroplaned dangerously. Most of the drivers had the good sense either to pull to the side of the road or slow down to a crawl. There were always exceptions, of course, and a few of them managed to wind up in ditches or in collisions with other vehicles.

The Reapers did what they could in their situation, which was find a motel, sit on their collective asses, and wait. Orologas had found new information on the destruction at the Four Horsemen clubhouse. He'd also spotted at least two other situations that might lead back to a creature hunting human beings. The "why" still remained a mystery.

Three bodies had been skinned in Boca Raton, but the work—while grisly—did not follow the MO they were looking for. The three had been a man, his wife, and their child. Horrifying, yes, but with the inclusion of a woman and an infant, it very likely wasn't the work of their quarry.

More promising, two men had been found in the Okefenokee, not far from the town where the Reapers were currently sitting on their laurels. While both bodies were in advanced stages of decomposition, and one of them showed evidence of being chewed on by an alligator, it didn't appear as if their deaths had been an accident. There was also a very real chance that whatever had done the killing had also taken trophies.

"You think this thing is going out in weather like this?"

"Hard to say," Orologas replied. "For all we know it loves it—this might be the alien version of a weekend in Cabo. We don't have enough information. Sure as hell wasn't raining like this in LA though."

They were in one of three rooms that they'd rented at the motel. The rooms were easily secured, and the clerk took cash. The only person he'd seen was Tomlin, who'd switched to civilian clothes before he made the arrangements. They'd paid for a week, and placed *Do Not Disturb* signs on the doors.

With luck they wouldn't use the rooms for more than a night, but seeing as they intended to stalk and capture an alien hunter, risking life and limb in the effort, it seemed a better notion than putting up tents in the middle of the swamp.

Orologas flipped his screen around to show everyone

the crime scene photos of the massacre at the bike club.

"So here's what we've got at the first scene," he said. "You can see there's around twelve bodies here, and most of them are mutilated in the extreme." They all leaned in closer to get a good look. It wasn't the sort of scene that added confidence to anyone's ego. Whatever had done the damage had torn bodies apart.

"Hunters are sick bastards," Hill said. "Especially the ones who do it for sport."

Tomlin nodded. "We don't know what the hell they're after, but if it's for fun and games, I'm going to enjoy taking this thing out."

King said nothing, but he stared at the images with nearly fanatical intensity. Then he pointed to an interior shot of the house, in what looked to be the main party room.

"There. Over there. Can you zoom in?" His finger touched the screen, Orologas leaned over to see what he was looking at, and then made adjustments. The image he wanted was the luminescent green puddle that spilled across part of the floor and onto the face of a dead man.

"What is that?"

"Might be the blood of that thing from what we've heard," King responded. "Pappy said they bleed green." He narrowed his eyes.

"Well, whatever color it bleeds, that's the color I want to see, and not ours," Tomlin said. "We don't know enough about this thing. It's big, and fast, and stealthy, and that's not nearly enough to go on."

Hill spoke up. "We know it kills. We know it took out a bunch of bikers."

"Well, if the thing's after the best we have to offer, he kind of missed the mark." Pulver's voice fairly dripped contempt.

Hill shook his head. "Don't get cocky. Back at Fort Benning I ran across a biker gang. Four dudes, none of them looked all that impressive, but they were ready for a fight and they held their own pretty damned good."

"Yeah? How many soldiers?" Orologas asked.

Hill looked at him and smiled, but he didn't answer.

"In any event, we need to get as ready as we can," Tomlin said. "Orologas, monitor the police channels. I want to hear about any possible disturbances, even with this storm going on."

The communications specialist nodded.

"Everyone else should try to get some rest while we still can." No one argued. Outside the rains kept hammering at the ground.

Now and then thunder let out a distant growl.

⚔ ⚔ ⚔

The war mask was not working as well as he wanted in the turbulent rain, so he took it off. His eyes would suffice in the current situation. The waters washed around his ankles, and with each surge of the wind the moisture crawled all the way up to his calves. The rains would not be stopping any time soon.

The dominant inhabitants of the planet seemed very nearly afraid of the weather, preferring to stay inside their domiciles rather than risk the moisture. To that end he decided to hunt other game.

The vast reptilian life forms within the wetlands

were not overly aggressive, but they were large and deadly. Within a few hours of reaching the area he had spotted the creatures and marked them as possible prey. Now that there was a chance to hunt them, he took advantage of it.

In the near darkness and the violent rains the things came closer to the surface, likely to look for fresh game. Even standing still at the edge of the water he could see them as they moved, sliding effortlessly through the currents, their eyes barely breaking the surface where they lurked. They had teeth and claws. Full-grown specimens had substantial body mass and prehensile tails that might even break his bones, if employed against him. The jaws of the creatures looked strong enough to bite through his leg, or even his torso.

Excellent.

Unlike the creatures with their firearms and their vehicles, these primitive beasts seemed like a proper threat. He wasn't foolish enough to doubt the dangerous nature of the dominants, however. He'd encountered them before, had hunted them, done battle with them and captured his prizes.

These were hunters, though—true hunters, carnivores that sought food. The thought made his blood surge and his pupils dilate. He let out a shuddering breath and waited patiently for one of the massive beasts to get close enough to provide a serious challenge.

He was not cloaked. This was a different sort of hunt. This was a personal battle against a target that was larger and physically superior to him. When one of them came for him, erupting from the waters in a sudden, violent charge, he reacted in kind.

The massive jaws of the beast slammed shut in the spot where his leg had been. He dodged the bite by a narrow margin and jumped back, preparing himself for combat. The creature was not so easily deterred, and came for him again, pushing its bulk onto the shore with surprising speed.

As he'd suspected, the tail of the reptile was a deadly weapon. The creature tried to strike using the heavy appendage, and he leaped over it, dropping down to the ground and then moving to the offensive before his opponent could reverse direction.

His claws met hard, scaled flesh and dug in, but not as deeply as he'd expected. The wounds he drew across the broad back of the thing were negligible. Then the powerful body shifted and sent him sprawling. So much faster than he'd expected. His senses were alert, and nervous energy coursed through him. He hit the ground and rolled himself away from the creature as it lunged and snapped its jaws and came for him yet again. How hungry it must be to risk leaving the waters. He did not understand the full nature of the thing, but had no doubt it preferred to remain submerged and safely hidden away.

It came again and for a moment panic caught inside of him. Truly the creature was massive. He'd chosen to fight it at close range, without any weapons, and watching as it lumbered his way he felt a flash of doubt. It was twice his length and it gave a booming hiss as it came for him.

Fear. It made him feel alive!

This was the joy of the hunt on its most primal level. His mouth opened and he bared teeth past quivering mandibles. Then his opponent's massive maw spread wide, and he understood the creature's weakness. It could see, but it could not see well when it was preparing to bite. He retreated again as the jaws slammed together a scant finger's distance from where he'd been standing. Had he not retreated, the creature would be feasting on his arm.

All the better!

This time when he attacked, he planted his heavy foot on the closed mouth of the thing and stomped down hard enough to feel the bones of the reptile's face break under his heel. Before it could respond he raked his claws across the thing's left eye and punctured the organ.

Half blinded and without a doubt in pain, the thing let out a deep, throaty roar and tried to retreat. As with many predators, if flight was an option the creature wanted to take it. But he did not intend to allow it.

The hunter attacked again, this time bringing his clawed foot down on the creature's back leg with enough force to bend the joint out of shape. Bone and cartilage shattered under the blow. Damaged and hindered in its attempt to escape, the reptile turned and charged in one ferocious motion. Teeth slammed down and raked across his leg. The pain was immediate and nearly incapacitating, but he had avoided the worst of the bite. The entire bulk of the thing came at him and rammed his body, staggering him.

The hunter hopped back on one uninjured leg and cursed his arrogance in thinking he might have an easy fight, even without his weapons. Still, his blood roared and his heart hammered in his chest as the thrill grew stronger. This was a fight! This was a hunt!

Another large hop backward and that mouth was opening again, the jaws parting to show teeth large enough to cut him as easily as his metal blades cut flesh. He lunged to its left side, where the creature was already blinded, and drove his claws into the scaled jaw, shredding flesh, carving through the muscles that controlled that deadly bite.

The head slapped in that direction and connected with his torso hard enough to throw him through the air. Had he not just torn the muscles on that side, the thing would surely have maimed him with the attempted bite. By the time he rose back to his feet the monster had almost made it back to the waters.

No. He would not lose his prize!

He grabbed the thick tail of the creature, grunted loudly, and braced and threw his full weight into bringing the beast back to him. At first it seemed to be rooted to the ground, and then the body was lifting into the air, even as its tail flexed and curled and took him off balance. He threw the beast even as it threw him.

The hunter landed in the muck at the edge of the water while his opponent rolled and slapped across the thick grass of the shoreline, shaking itself violently. For a moment the hunter's vision doubled, but he stood just the same, crouching into a battle-ready stance as he shook away the second reptile that mirrored the first.

He placed himself between the beast and its watery

retreat. It came for him again, croaking out a deep roar and charging, heavy body low to the ground and tail slashing the foliage behind it as it rushed forward.

The mouth could not open properly. It could not attack with a bite, and would likely never be able to eat again.

He stepped to the left side, out of the path of his prey, and drove his foot into the muscles behind that heavy head, then cut a deep trench with his claws, dragging them forward across the same area and cutting deeper into the meat. When the reptile whipped its body around to attack, its movements were sluggish. It might be feigning a deeper injury, though he doubted the creature had the intelligence to manage that.

As it twisted its heavy body, he dropped onto the creature's back and caught the mangled jaw with his hands. It reared up, and he wrapped his thick legs around its heavy belly, tightening his grip to prevent the wounded jaw from opening again.

The fight was not yet done, however. The thing rolled its body, thrashing violently against the ground in an effort to dislodge him. His legs constricted around that middle and his arms held tightly to the wounded jaw, keeping it closed. The impact of the thing's body slamming him into the ground was brutal, but not enough to shake him loose.

His legs squeezed and he hooked his feet together to make sure his grip did not slip. His arms locked tighter still and he wrenched the head sideways with all the strength he could muster. Once, a second time, and then a third. On the fourth attempt he felt bones in the neck slide, and then separate.

As the body thrashed with less and less force, he maintained his grip. His face was half submerged in a puddle when the beast finally breathed its last, shuddered, and died. He stayed that way for a long while, breathing carefully and savoring the feel of killing an enemy he had not been certain he could defeat.

When he rose to his feet again he saw the damage to his thigh—the scrapes where he had come very close to losing several important muscles. The rain washed the bloody wound as he worked on gathering his trophies. The head of the beast, the spine of the beast, and the clawed forefeet as well. This was a prize he would long remember.

The rains kept coming as he headed for his ship to properly clean and tend to his wounds and get a night's rest. This encounter had inspired him, and he looked forward to the greater hunts that were still to come.

He felt it with every fiber of his being.

There would be a glorious hunt soon.

10

The clouds stayed where they were, but at least the rain calmed down. Traeger took a quick shower, pulled out a fresh suit and got himself to work. The next meeting of the subcommittee was only a day away and he had a lot to do between now and then. It could decide the fate of Project Stargazer.

The good news? The Reapers were actively pursuing a target. From what he'd been told the night before, it was looking very promising.

"So how do we spin this?" he asked his reflection as he lathered up his cheeks and chin for a close shave. "Say it's happening now? Maybe a little lie?" he shrugged. "I mean, very little, because those boys are damned good."

Which was true. Every mission they'd taken only made him look better in the eyes of the Agency. That helped, but it wasn't enough. If he wanted to make sure the project stayed alive, and that he gained certain benefits at the same time, he'd have to stretch the truth somewhat and hope it didn't blow up in his face.

That decided, he finished getting himself ready and left the quarters he'd been assigned.

This likely was an easy task. All it required was that the right palms be greased, and he'd already made steps in that direction. He'd prepared the way for several players to help him gain the financial strength the project would need. Now the challenging part came—convincing those players to pull the trigger. He didn't think he'd have too much trouble, though some of them were likely to play hard to get unless he damned near promised them the world.

First on the list was Carl Whelan. The man owned a company that specialized in the sort of technology no one ever thought about—construction and mining and heavy equipment for changing the shape of the planet one step at a time. Since no one ever thought about that sort of thing, Whelan had nearly monopolized the market. He had the cash flow to help Traeger, and in return he would be promised a boost to his technologies that would give him an incontrovertible edge—provided, of course, that the technologies could be gleaned from whatever the Reapers could acquire.

N N N

They met for breakfast at a diner that offered the most amazing omelets he'd ever tasted, and charged dearly for the privilege of consuming them. Whelan ate his with hard little strokes of his fork, followed by vicious mastication once the food was in his mouth. Traeger could imagine the man crushing his enemies with the exact same sort of relish.

Whelan listened intently while Traeger made his pitch, both of them using the appropriate level of caution to ensure that anyone close by and too curious would have no idea whatsoever what was being discussed.

"You need funding. I need assurances." Whelan spoke over a steaming cup of black coffee, then took a sip of it. It looked damned close to boiling temperature, but if he felt any discomfort, he hid it well.

"Well, I can't give you anything in writing," Traeger said. "I'm sure you understand."

"Then what can you give me?"

"What do you want?"

"That's a list that could go on for days." The man's smile was as predatory as a shark's and his eyes were almost as cold.

"Let's try this a different way." Traeger weighed the possibilities, and then leaned forward with a smile of his own. "What will it take for you to throw your cards in?"

"Well, now…" Whelan almost purred. "You're in the information business. Aside from the concessions you've already discussed, I'd like a little information."

That was exactly what Traeger had hoped the man would say.

"Which of your competitors did you want to know about?"

He slid the list across the table, and Traeger took it. The paper was folded and he left it that way. There would be time for considering the situation—and the request— after the meal. There was no need for a handshake. They finished the meal without any further talk, but it was companionable silence. When Traeger reached for the check, Whelan beat him to it and smiled.

"A pleasure doing business with you, William."

"Likewise." He smiled back.

Victory tasted even better than the omelet.

N N N

Woodhurst sighed. The meetings were continuing, and they were going better than he'd hoped, but they still weren't going as well as he needed them to go. Even the news that the team was on the hunt wasn't enough to grease the wheels as much as he'd have liked.

Somewhere out there, Traeger was doing his best— allegedly—and the general hoped it was enough, though he hated the very concept. He still had a problem with Traeger. He just didn't trust him. The man was as slick as a politician, and he was the kind of person who would stop at nothing to get what he wanted. At least the politicians of the world—most of them, anyhow— were smart enough to worry about getting caught with their hands in the cookie jar on one side, and the mud on the other.

Traeger seemed like the sort who would make sure that if he was caught doing anything wrong, no one would ever talk about it. They were both on the same side, and sometimes the man could accomplish miraculous things, but he seemed to enjoy the work more than Woodhurst thought he should.

It was just a feeling. Still, he'd spent a lifetime of dealing with vipers clothed in human flesh.

The phone buzzed. It was Elliott. *Good*. He was between meetings and wanted some sort of good news.

"What's new, Pappy?"

The man knew better than to give a straight answer. No matter what anyone claimed about cell phone security, he was an agent of the CIA, and therefore came with a certain level of built-in paranoia.

"Not too much to say yet, General," Elliott replied. "Just that the news so far is good."

"No acquisitions yet? No contact?"

"Not so far, but it looks as if we're heading in the right direction. Every sign says so."

Woodhurst shook his head. He didn't want an update unless it indicated progress. He wanted to hear that they'd had success, that there was concrete evidence to present to the people with whom he was meeting—the very people who would decide the fate of his project.

But he didn't want to rain on Elliott's parade.

"Keep me posted, Pappy," he said. "Good luck to everyone."

He killed the call.

Pappy Elliott was stressed—he could tell. The man wanted this done, too. He wanted the alien caught, and maybe even more than Woodhurst did. That said a great deal.

The Reapers were likely even more desperate than their leaders. They'd been yanked, one and all, from assignments that promised advancement, and had been training for more than a year. Once rising stàrs, now they barely existed in the eyes of the military they'd enlisted to serve. Were they frustrated? Like a boy going solo to his prom.

And they were likely just as desperate.

The next meeting was still fifteen minutes out, but at a different location. Woodhurst stood up and headed for the door. The check had already been paid. He just needed to get to a bar two blocks away. If it took him more than ten minutes to walk a couple of blocks, he'd be retiring inside of a week.

The sky was beginning to clear, and the temperature had dropped by several degrees, making it uncannily comfortable for the District of Columbia. If there had been an alien in DC, it likely would have headed for a different hunting ground.

Woodhurst smiled to himself and shook his head. What a notion. As far as the general was concerned some of the deadliest creatures on the planet could be found at the local bars, and more of them were in the House of Representatives and on the senate floor.

◢ ◢ ◢

The rains slowed down, but did not go away. Just the same, the Reapers left the hotel and stowed their equipment properly in the two vehicles they were driving—a van and an SUV. Both were nondescript, and well-secured. The average car thief trying to break in would be hard pressed to manage to pick the locks, and the windows were bulletproof.

Better safe than sorry.

No new details had come to light, but that fact didn't

stop the group from heading out. One and all, they weren't comfortable waiting for something to happen—not when they could be out hunting, or at least getting the lay of the land.

Anything they did had to be based on news reports and police broadcasts. To that end Orologas was the busiest of them. While most of the Reapers sat in their seats and looked out at the streets, he listened to the police scanner and checked for activity that might reflect more of the same sort of carnage.

"They always make this look so easy in the movies." Orologas was talking to himself, but Hill rolled his eyes.

"No such thing as the easy way." Hill looked out the windows at the trees on one side and the small houses on the other. There was a whole lot of nothing worth seeing, as far as he was concerned. He sighed and mentally agreed with the communications specialist.

Then he was all attention.

"Might have something." Orologas spoke softly and held up a hand to show that he wasn't ready with anything just yet. "Sounds like a raid on a crack house." Orologas shrugged. "Might be worth checking out. There will be people with weapons and attitude problems."

"Sounds like wishful thinking to me." Hill chuckled.

"Agreed." Tomlin nodded. "But let's check it out anyway. Stay discreet, though."

11

Hampstead Road ended in a cul-de-sac with six houses in a semicircle. Each of those houses was a single-story ranch style made of brick and looked enough like the one next to it that the only way to tell them apart came from the lawn decorations, or lack thereof. Those, and the color of the wood trim.

They'd all been built in the nineteen sixties and were in decent repair, but they were nothing to write home about. The proper description was, frankly, "nondescript," and that was exactly the idea.

The rains had slowed but not gone away, and the lawns around the houses were marked with pockets of standing water, some several inches deep.

The first squad car rolled down the street at just after ten in the morning, and Tuey—the kid they paid to be a lookout—did his job perfectly. He pushed two fingers into his mouth and blew out a loud, shrill whistle that would have shaved the life off anyone standing too close to him.

Nick Lamden did what he was supposed to do and dropped the meth into the safe they'd installed under the rug in the living room, then hauled the coffee table over the rug. They might find the shit, but they'd be hard pressed to get the safe open, especially while he was alive. He intended to live through it, though, 'cause his momma didn't raise any fools.

While Nick was busy hiding the meth, his brother Jamie slid the money into the deposit bag from the local bank and took off out the back door before the cops even thought about tapping their brakes outside the house. He was long and lean and ran track back in high school and during his two years of college. Never a gold medalist type, he made second place enough times that everyone trusted him to know how to move his ass. He was probably out of the neighborhood before the first cop set foot on the sidewalk.

There were three others in the place, Nick knew, and they were all armed. There were a few surprises in the area, too—seven other guys in the surrounding houses who were there solely to help keep things running smoothly.

He couldn't figure out who might have tipped off the cops, but he'd figure it out later. Nick hadn't built up his little empire to have it destroyed by some asshole trying to cut a deal with the local authorities, and he'd sure as hell get to the bottom of it, soon as he was finished with business.

While his brother booked down the back roads, Nick strapped on his bulletproof vest. The black-and-whites kept coming, and a massive armored van with "S.W.A.T" written on the side blocked off any easy route of escape.

That was okay. He had plenty of backup, and getting anything at all out of him or his associates was going to be a hell of a challenge.

Despite his bravado, his hands were shaking with an adrenaline kick, and his heart was going twice as fast as it normally did.

Oh yeah, this was scary shit.

"Nick. We got more cops coming, man." Jorge sounded like he was ready to piss himself. Nick knew how he felt. "They got guns."

"No shit," Nick replied. "We got vests and bigger guns, man. Let's do this."

The houses on the street were all the property of El Corazon Holding, a company he'd made up five years earlier. The people living there got to stay for free and they got paid besides. Their loyalty was easy. They had nowhere else to go and he was the man taking care of their bills.

"Jorge, get Red on the phone, tell him to start shooting as soon as they reach the door," Nick said, talking fast. "Before they knock. I *mean* it."

Jorge didn't hesitate. He was on the cell in seconds, and talking in hushed tones.

While they were waiting the cops got closer, carrying their own assault rifles, sporting their own body armor and walking with a very large battering ram to knock down the door. It was a reinforced fire door with a thin plywood veneer. It'd take a few hits, and by the time the cops figured that out, the plan was for them to be shredded wheat courtesy of Red and the other neighborhood gunmen.

Jorge kept speaking as the police came closer.

And then all hell broke loose.

Red started firing, and the cops went scattering in all directions, taken off guard by the extra firepower from across the street. Red was a stand-up guy and an ex-marine. He took his time and aimed for each cop before he fired. His first round hit a SWAT dude in the area just to the left of the vest he was wearing and blew away a large portion of the poor bastard's arm. He spun hard and fell to the ground.

By the time the cops realized one of theirs had been shot, Red had aimed and fired a second time. His aim wasn't flawless. He caught the second target in the chest and knocked the man backward a good four feet, but it didn't look like the bullet went through the armor.

Nick picked up his weapon of choice and Jorge picked up the street sweeper he'd been fantasizing about using since they were in middle school. The weapon fired ten rounds from a drum before being emptied. Jorge had fired the thing at a range once and nearly deafened everyone, despite the fact that they were wearing ear protection. He'd also blown the entire target into shreds.

No one opened the door. They didn't need to, not yet at least. The cops were too busy running like rabbits. Nick didn't laugh, didn't find anything particularly funny in the situation. Instead he just watched as the events unfolded.

Despite the constant drizzle he could see Red clearly from across the street. The man was up on the top of his house, lying in a prone position and taking careful aim. He was hidden well enough that most people looking from street level wouldn't see him. Nick had the advantage of knowing where Red's special hiding spot was, and of being at a different angle than anyone on the street. He could see the man's head and shoulders and the rifle he was aiming.

So he got to watch when something slightly larger than a cup saucer tore through the air and took off the top of Red's head. Sliced through him like a hot wire through a stick of butter, and kept going with barely a waver in its trajectory. The shimmering thing sailed past and then returned along its own path, turning fast and hard and going right past Red even as he flopped across the roof in a growing pool of blood and gray matter.

"What the fuck was that?" Nick stared at Red's corpse. It wasn't the cops—they were all still trying to decide where they should take cover in an area where they were surrounded by houses.

Jorge looked his way and shrugged.

"What was what?"

"Something just killed Red."

"Say what?" Jorge stared at the roof. "I can't see him."

"He's *dead*," Nick shouted. "Something cut his fucking head open."

"You've gotta be shittin' me."

"Just watch out the window," Nick said angrily, "and see what's coming our way." He didn't have time to play twenty questions.

One of the cops took a shot at the roof, thinking he had a target up there, and caught nothing but air. An instant later the man's leg was vaporized by a blast of what looked like a high-velocity glow stick. The impact was enough to send the cop sailing up and away from where he'd been standing.

Jorge saw that, and let out a shocked squawk.

"What the hell did that?"

"Fuck if I know," Nick responded.

Another of the cops fell, screaming bloody murder as bits and pieces of his flesh sprayed halfway across the squad car next to him. The screams only lasted for a second.

Then the police went crazy. They tried to aim everywhere at once. It sounded like someone was yelling out commands, but Nick couldn't hear what the guy was saying. He could only watch while they did their best to find cover, pull the one-legged cop to safety, and spot whatever the hell was cutting them down.

Someone popped out of the front door under where Red had been. It was Curtis, who was one of the crazier people he had working for him. Curtis had decided to make a run for it, carrying a pistol in each hand, and he was hunkered over as he bolted for the next house in the cul-de-sac.

Clay pigeons would have had an easier time at a skeet-shooting convention. Several of the cops took time away from the chaos to draw weapons and take aim, a couple of them bellowing commands that came through closed windows as muffled, incoherent noises. It wasn't hard to figure out what they were shouting, though.

That idiot Curtis chose to do exactly what he shouldn't have done, and took aim at the closest officer. He never got to pull the trigger. Several very jumpy cops opened fire, all at the same time. More than being shot, Curtis was torn apart. The sight of his shredded body would stay with Nick for as long as he lived—however long that might be.

Then he saw what the rest of them couldn't. While they were gunning Curtis down, something killed two more of the cops. Nick couldn't actually say what happened. There was a flare of light, and one of the SWAT members got knocked back three feet by an impact from something that wasn't there. At the same time, that silvery object he'd seen before cleaved through the chest of another cop, sliding through his armored torso in a stream of blood and entrails.

That was when Nick decided to hit the deck. The police were losing their shit, and whatever was going on out there was only going to get worse. Over his head a bunch of shots came tearing through the window. It was inevitable, really—the cops must've figured he was responsible for the guys who got cut down, and they did what anyone would do. They went a little crazy.

The barrage seemed to last forever.

Jorge was down on the floor not far away, his hands over his head and his face pressed into the shag carpet. He looked terrified, and Nick thought he might have pissed his pants.

"What the fuck was that?" Jorge's voice was high and hoarse.

"That was the goddamn cops trying to kill us." His voice shook more than he'd expected, and adrenaline was kicking his heart into overdrive. It didn't make him feel like fighting, though. Nick just wanted this done. He wanted out. He wanted to live. Hell, he had enough money stashed away that he could get out of the business if he wanted. Maybe even go straight.

He wanted that a lot right then.

"No, not the fucking cops—the *other* thing." Jorge shook his head. "There's something out there killing cops."

As if to prove his point another round of bullets tore into the side of the house. Fragments of glass sprayed into the room, along with shards of wood from the window frame as it disintegrated under the barrage. Nick could feel the fragments that littered his clothes and wormed their way into his hair down to the scalp. He could hear the cops now as they screamed out commands to each other. Someone called out the name "Simpson."

The gunfire continued, but it was aimed elsewhere, and he breathed a very small sigh of relief. They must've realized it was someone out there picking them off. They had to know that the shots weren't coming from the house. They had to.

Please, God, they have to.

"There it is!"

"What the hell are you talking about?" Nick demanded.

"I saw it," Jorge insisted. "It's like a chameleon. You can only see it when it moves, but it's up there, on the roof."

"Well it can stay up there—long as it doesn't get anywhere near us," Nick said. "Maybe it'll kill all the cops for us."

"It's moved." Jorge rose up to his knees and looked out the window, squinting. "I don't know where it is now." No one blew his head off his shoulders, which Nick thought was a miracle. Then he got brave, and lifted himself high enough to look out the window and see where the cops were. Flashing red and blue lights made the scene even more surreal.

There were ten or twelve of them now, maybe more in hiding. They were still all over the place, a few of them attempting to tend their wounded and others looking around with jerky motions, trying to see what might be hunting them even as they crouched behind cars or duckwalked around. Nick watched them and shook his head. They were almost funny, except that their fear was real, and likely to get him killed if he wasn't careful.

That flash of light again.

A man in uniform lost an arm.

All around the falling man people ran, and bellowed, and looked for the source of the assault. One of them seemed to get a break. He pointed and fired, and something big moved from the roof. A distorted shape, it landed on the ground and charged toward the shooter. Nick couldn't quite see it, only the flashes of warped scenery that it passed as it moved.

The shooter backpedaled like crazy, his face a mask of terror. He took aim to fire again and the thing—big, it was big and it was fast—dodged to the side, then came up as the cop fired. It was close and it hit him hard. The cop sailed backward, and whatever it had hit him with shredded the front of the man's vest, the uniform beneath, and the flesh under that.

Blood sprayed everywhere.

That was all it took.

The cops quit firing wildly. They focused their

gunfire on the spot where the cop had been hit. Then they stopped—probably to assess the damage—and everything went weirdly silent.

Nick's phone rang, and he squealed like a little girl.

Caller ID said it was Tony DeMatteis. Tony was across the street, and probably wanted to know what the plan was. Fuck, there was no plan. That was the problem. He needed to think of something to fix this.

Outside, another cop let out a scream and soared into the air, spiraling as he ascended. The man's face was gone, just a bloody pulp, and the blood spiraled with him. Someone fired where he had been and managed to shoot the flashing light off one of the squad cars instead of hitting anything they might have been aiming for.

Then someone got lucky. That was all there was to it. One of the police officers fired at something that Nick didn't see, and suddenly there was a flickering run of colors in the air that sputtered and grew into a solid form.

The thing stood easily seven feet in height, and while it was human in shape, it sure as hell wasn't human. The body was broad and heavily muscled, with a metal mask over its face and what looked like dreadlocks or maybe snakes instead of hair. Whatever might be going on under that mask, no one would ever be able to guess, but Nick was okay with that because the rest of that body, well, it was the sort of thing he never wanted to see exposed.

The skin he *could* see was mottled. A dull greenish hue in spots, but with heavy darker areas that made him think of a few lizards he'd seen at the zoo. He had no idea if that skin was natural or if the thing was wearing some sort of padding. He couldn't tell from his range and had no intention of getting any closer.

It was like someone had mixed too many things together. The thing wore what looked like a loincloth worthy of Tarzan, but along with the metal faceplate it also had armor on different parts of the body, covering the shins and knees and partially covering the thighs, and there was armor on one side of the creature's ribs that ran up to one shoulder. On that shoulder there was something that looked, well, *dangerous* was the only way he could think of it. Not like a weapon he could understand, but the way that thing moved, it made him think of artillery on a ship.

Just to prove his point, the thing shifted and the same sort of burning light he'd seen before erupted from what looked like a small cannon. The light hit one of the cops and blew a hole through the poor bastard's entire chest and back. He was dead way before he hit the ground.

There were gauntlets on the creature's wrists, and one of them had heavy blades. The other hand held a metal rod that telescoped onto a very pointy and deadly looking spear. He saw all of that at the same time that the police did, and suddenly they were all focused on the nightmare thing that was moving through them, knocking people aside like they weighed nothing at all.

"Fuck it." He stood up and headed toward the back door. "Jorge, let's get the hell out of here." He didn't have to say it twice. The man barreled across the room and Nick followed. The cops were busy getting killed, and that was a mighty fine distraction to help them avoid getting shot or arrested.

Three paces outside the door Jorge came to a stop and held his hands over his head. Nick charged out behind him and started swinging his pistol around, ready to open fire.

Eight armed guys immediately made him change his mind. One of them took a fast step in Nick's direction and brought the butt end of a rifle across his face.

Nick dropped to the ground, unconscious.

12

"Drag him inside. We don't need anyone seeing this and wondering what happened." Tomlin shook his head. He'd have preferred that they be subdued and taken in under their own power, but some things couldn't be helped. In the same situation he'd have done exactly what Hyde did.

At least the other one was conscious and standing with his hands over his head. He pointed to the man.

"Get your ass in the house."

The man damned near ran inside, and they followed. The place was torn up, with bullet holes running through several walls and the windows in the front of the house completely shattered.

"It's worse than we thought," Tomlin growled. He turned to the rest. "We go out the back again, and we spread out. Hill, take Strand, Hyde, and Pulver. The rest of you are on me." He looked at the man still standing there, and shook his head. "You want to run, you run, but do not get in our way or I'll kill you myself—is that clear?"

The man nodded as hard as a bobblehead in an earthquake. Tomlin took the guy's weapons, and he bolted through the back door. Tomlin motioned, and they all followed him out.

Heading to the right, they moved around the building and observed the melee taking place in the center of the cul-de-sac. There were bodies strewn across the pavement, some intact and others torn apart. For a moment he saw the alien hunter, a massive shape that towered over the largest man he'd ever seen. And then, as if he were looking at a mirage, it flickered and faded away.

"Shit! It's gone stealth!" His words weren't meant for anyone but him, but the rest of his team heard them. They grew even more alert, and spread out. King crouched lower to the ground and got a better grip on his weapon.

One of the SWAT team members took a running start and hit something in the still air. The man's body came to an abrupt stop, and whatever he'd hit let out a chittering roar, and then cut the guy in two. Blood and bone and meat exploded out of the man's back and his head imploded from the force of the strike.

That was enough for Tomlin. Lifting his rifle he aimed roughly a foot above the dead man and fired. He was rewarded with a roar of what he hoped was pain, and then the creature was charging. It covered half the ground between them in seconds, and then stopped, the head moving slowly. At first Tomlin could only see an odd ripple in the air, a sign that something was there, even if it was not clearly seen.

The thing that had vanished into nothing reappeared, whatever sort of cloaking technology it used flickering as it looked around. The face was still hidden behind a metal mask, and from that mask three small red beams of light cut across the misty air and headed for Tomlin. He did the only sensible thing.

He dropped and rolled.

An instant later the side of the building where he'd been crouched was vaporized, shredded in an explosion that shattered brick and turned wood into toothpick-sized projectiles. Several small shards rained across him, and a few cut into his arm and scalp as he came up from his rolling maneuver and kept moving.

A second blast hit the spot where he'd been only a second before and sent Tomlin sailing backward. He hit the lawn hard enough to tear the turf apart, and stared at the sky for a moment, trying hard to remember his name, why he was there, whichever came first.

While he was lying dazed on the ground, Orologas took aim with his Ithaca and fired a stun round at the thing trying to end Tomlin's world. The hard rubber bullet rolled and soared and hit the creature in the shoulder as it tried to dodge away. Nothing was fast enough to actually dodge a slug fired from a shotgun, but it tried and almost succeeded.

Almost didn't count. The thing stepped back, staggered as the bullet hit the metal shoulder mount on its left side. The head snapped around quickly to look at Orologas and before he could pump a second round into the Ithaca's chamber, the alien threw something at him.

They'd been pressed hard to train and keep training, until physical responses were motor memory and bordered on instinct. Orologas backed up and blocked with his shotgun, which was the only thing that saved his life. The rounded disc cut through the air and then through the stock of the Ithaca, slowed just enough by the impact that Orologas managed to drop backward before it could carve its way through him.

The man looked at the halves of his shotgun and immediately threw them down. The non-lethal approach hadn't even come close. He needed a different weapon.

While he scrambled for one the rest of the Reapers went into action. King also tried the non-lethal approach, and fired the twin needles of his Taser into the creature's heavily muscled torso. The voltage in a Taser was designed to overwhelm brain activity, immediately incapacitating the target for as long as the current continued to move through the cables. It hurt like hell too.

A clicking sound indicated the Taser at work. The alien let loose a warbling scream and stood perfectly still.

King's lips pulled up in a tight grin.

While the creature was frozen in agony, Hill fired. They wanted the thing alive, so the shot was meant to be non-lethal. Killing was an option, though. The bullet caught the alien in the chest, but only did minor damage. The creature's metal armor was placed strategically and saved it from a more severe injury. The hole that was pounded into the thing's torso was small at the entry point, and likely at the exit too.

As the rest of the team moved in, the disc that had taken out Orologas's shotgun came back around in a wide arc, and whether it was controlled by the alien or the aim was simple luck, the edge on the whirring disc sliced through his left arm and part of his chest. Orologas never made a sound as he fell to his knees and then flat on his face.

Strand called out the man's name and moved three paces toward his fellow soldier before he turned and, cursing loudly, aimed at the alien. His shot was spot on. The bullet struck the metal faceplate and left a deep trench in the area just above the eyes, knocking the creature backward with the force of the blow.

The flying disc turned. Crawling to his hands and knees, Tomlin saw it. The damned thing shifted in midflight and cut through the Taser's cables. The creature tore the barbs from its chest and immediately aimed the shoulder-mounted cannon at King.

King bolted, running hard and fast to avoid being an easy target.

The alien shot anyway, and did a fine job of guessing where its target would be. The shot caught the man in the chest and tore him apart before he could clear ten paces.

Still on his knees, Tomlin rose, moving fast from there. He sighted and fired, aiming for the alien's chest. His shot punched through the surface but didn't go very far. The bone density of the thing must have been epic, because the bullet was stopped without exiting.

That didn't make the creature any happier.

N N N

They came out from behind the structures and swarmed like vermin. He saw them and knew they were different. The group he had nearly finished was trained, and bore weapons, but lacked cohesion. The fact that they were not expecting him was relatively insignificant.

When he'd happened across the gathering forces, he initially meant to merely observe the two rival warring factions, but instead had chosen to add chaos to the mix—the better to hunt the strongest of the warriors among the species. There were some in his clan who would have accused him of provoking a response from both groups. He wouldn't have disagreed, but found their reactions to the unexpected attacks exhilarating. They were the most dangerous when cornered.

Yet they offered less challenge than he'd hoped.

Nevertheless, the species here was good sport. They weren't quick to surrender, and they were capable of causing substantial damage given the proper motivation. When the melee finally started and he began killing his prey, he let himself get sloppy. He forgot to check his periphery as carefully as he should have.

That was when the new faction joined the hunt. The team gathering between the domiciles was more cohesive, well-armed, and not as likely to flee. Better prey than the ones he had fought, they came out shooting. The difference was apparent. They weren't trying to kill others of their own species.

They were hunting for him.

His pulse slammed into a higher rate and he

immediately forgot the lesser hunters he had been killing. They were, as a whole, damaged or dying. The prey remaining inside their domiciles were not a threat. He could see that in most cases they had already prepared to flee, and some had already fled the area, retreating rather than engaging in conflict. Cowards.

These new participants, however, were a different sort. They worked together as a unit, or rather they tried. His first assault must have incapacitated a leader of the group because the rest immediately moved to protect their downed compatriot while simultaneously they sought to attack him.

Weapons were fired as he cloaked himself, moving closer. One of the prey managed to hit his gauntlet, and though no substantial damage seemed to occur, his cloak was shut off an instant later.

There were eight of them. He needed to move quickly if he was going to stop them.

While the first was still recovering, several more came for him, firing their weapons with varying levels of success. It took him only a moment to understand that they were either very bad at aiming, or they were attempting to subdue rather than kill him. That was a mistake. As his chieftain had said many times when the hunts began, *"Hunting is a serious task and cannot be done without proper dedication to the slaying of targets."*

They wanted to play at hunting. He sought to hunt and collect his trophies.

The first shot that struck him was painful, but left no mark. He threw his disc and cut down one of the would-be hunters. Another of them incapacitated him with a high-voltage charge, then was killed by a blast of plasma. The remote control for the disc was located in his well-insulated face plate, and worked well enough that he could cut the cables holding him.

The second shot bored a hole in his chest that was small, and barely bled. The third bounced off his faceplate instead of penetrating, then another projectile hit his chest. It lodged in his rib and was painful.

Enough of the games.

He charged, moving for the one that had shot him last, even as the creature scrambled from its semi-prone position and prepared to defend itself.

They came for him as one, perfectly willing to engage in close-quarters combat. That was for the best, as he could do little to avoid their ranged weapons except move to where those devices could not be so easily aimed. Up close, he pushed the wrist blades from his gauntlet and drew the Combistick from his belt. The stick telescoped to its full length even as he used it to strike the one that had shot him in the ribs.

The human almost avoided the blow, and rolled to disperse the worst of the kinetic force. He was impressed. When struck, most of them simply fell down and bled out. This one had armor and skill to aid in surviving.

One of the darker-skinned members of the assault team came for him, a heavy blade in its hand. He blocked the blade with his gauntlet and pushed the fighter back with all of his weight. The man rolled away in an uncontrolled stagger and crashed into the closest structure hard enough to draw blood from the back of its head.

The rest tried to swarm him, moving as one, calling to each other in their odd gibberish language and trying to overwhelm him with sheer numbers. It was an excellent strategy but one that would not succeed.

The Combistick caught one of the fools in the abdomen and punched through the armor with ease. The thing thrashed and screeched, dropping the bludgeon it had planned to use on him. He swept his arm to the right and sent two more of the creatures stumbling back. The problem they faced was simple—they were worried about hurting one another, and he did not care if any of them were injured.

They were all going to die under any circumstances.

∦ ∦ ∦

Tomlin wasn't down, but it was close. Hill was staggered and dizzy and, despite the bashing he'd taken already, he decided it was time to take charge. There wasn't a plan in it for advancement, just a need to see things done.

He pointed to Strand and told him to flank the damned thing. Strand didn't hesitate. The cattle prod was fully charged and when he struck the alien the thing let out another warbling scream and turned its attention to its latest attacker.

Before it could respond, he gestured for Burke to hit the thing hard. Never even blinked. He just lifted his street sweeper and unloaded four of the rubber shells into the thing's back and side, running in a half-circle as he fired. These were a larger shell. Each of the thunderous discharges hit the creature and sent it stumbling. It let out a roar as it dropped to its knees.

Any thought that it might be incapacitated disappeared when it caught Burke's arm in a grip and pulled him closer. Burke was cocking the shotgun, but never had a chance to pull the trigger before the heavy metal blades on the creature's left wrist severed his arm above and below the elbow.

Burke let out a scream and backed away, blood vomiting from the wound in his upper arm. He was dead. There was no chance in hell that anyone was going to be able to stop the blood flow, and Hill knew it. It'd be a miracle if the guy made it back to Stargazer.

Strand tried again with the cattle prod, but only managed to get it blocked and then knocked aside by the metal spear the thing was holding. Instead of retreating, Strand stepped forward and drove his elbow into the giant's throat.

The creature gagged and coughed and grabbed Strand's head in one massive hand before driving an armored knee into the poor bastard's face. Strand hit the ground with all the grace of a sack of rocks, his features bloodied and misshapen.

Tomlin was back up and aiming at the creature again. Hill stepped in closer and threw a smoke grenade at the damned thing just to confuse it.

The creature ignored the smoke. Whatever that helmet did, it must have given it a clean view and enabled it to breathe. Various reports had stated that the alien hunters could see in the infrared spectrum, and maybe even in other spectrums as well. Even so, he'd hoped the smoke might distract it a bit.

Instead the thing rose to its full height and pointed the sharp end of its stick right at Hill's face.

That was okay. When he was growing up, his old man always said, *"The best way not to get hit is to not be where your enemy is swinging."* The first thrust found air. So did the second. When the third came his way Hill dodged to the side again and caught the other end of the damned stick across his shoulder. Big as the thing was, it was fast, too. It spun the staff around and nailed him before he could recover.

Pulver hit the thing in the side with a dart that was supposed to have enough juice in it to knock out a whale. The shot was true. The heavy gauge needle stuck out of the monster's side and quivered.

It looked at the needle, and then over at Pulver. While it did, Jermaine Hyde did what he did best and came in for a sneak attack.

The man was as fast as anyone Hill had ever seen, and he was quiet besides. There were no slouches in the Reapers, but Hyde scared him just a little. He wrapped his arms around the creature's thick neck, right at what had to be a vulnerable spot, between the mask and the thick collar the creature wore. In that narrow gap, Hyde wrapped a heavy cord between his hands and then dropped backward.

The thing shook, and reached, and tried to grab at Hyde, but the man avoided its attempts and dropped lower still.

The creature turned, trying to find easy access to its attacker, but instead of giving up his advantage, Hyde actually stepped up the monster's leg and then wrapped himself around the thick, muscular waist, his legs scissoring together to get a firm grip and apply pressure to the vulnerable parts of the creature's midsection. Caught around the waist and the neck, the alien hunter spun, trying to find its enemy and failing.

Hyde held on like a man fighting against a bucking bronco. He managed to keep his grip despite the odds.

Damn...

While Hyde fought to stay exactly where he was, and to cut off the blood flow to the behemoth's brain, Pulver nailed it again and again with the darts from his tranquilizer gun. Tomlin stood next to Hill and kept his weapon aimed at the thing, but ultimately it didn't matter. He never had to fire it.

The monster they'd hunted staggered, and then slowly fell backward, landing on Hyde as it crashed to the ground.

Tomlin looked to Hill.

"You're bleeding."

Hill nodded and felt the massive wet spot on the back of his head. "Yeah. Fucker hit me with a house." He looked at Tomlin and saw several lacerations. "You ain't looking whole yourself."

"We have to get this done." He looked at the creature. Even as they watched Hyde was working, moving out from under the heavy form and quickly applying inch-thick zip ties to the thing's heavy wrists and ankles. Hill nodded and winced.

"Not gonna be long before someone comes around. I'll go get the van."

Tomlin shook his head. "No. That's a nasty wound. You might have a concussion." He pointed to Pulver. "The van, Kyle."

Pulver nodded and Hill tossed him the keys. There was no more talk. They worked as quickly as they could to finish binding the oversized nightmare that had taken out four of the team with ease.

Tomlin addressed the fallen, going from member to member and quickly gathering their tags. Two dead, two badly wounded.

Hill and Hyde made sure the restraints were solid and then Hill did his best to disable whatever weapons he could find on the creature. Mostly that meant peeling parts off and setting them aside. Two gauntlets and the shoulder mount were stripped away before the van arrived. The mask could wait for later. For all they knew the fucker would suffocate in the atmosphere, and he wasn't taking any chances. General Woodhurst wanted the thing alive. Pappy wanted the thing alive.

That was enough for him.

Tomlin looked around like he'd been punched in the head a few too many times and Hill understood.

They'd won. They'd captured an actual Off World Life Form.

All it had cost them was half the Reapers in exchange.

Some people were going to look at that as a victory.

Tomlin was not. He'd lost men under his command and that hurt. Hill knew, because even though the command wasn't his, he felt the blow just as deeply.

13

"They're coming home with a prize."

Jerry Entwhistle's message was short and crisp. That was all Pappy needed to hear. It was enough.

It was too much.

Elliott sat down on the corner of his desk and stared at his hands. They'd been younger hands once, and they'd been powerful. He could look at them now and see the scars from a dozen conflicts that had aged him long before time had gotten hold of him. The one scar that he always saw, no matter whether he wanted to see it or hide from it, was one of the smallest. A dimpled mass that ran through the web between the forefinger and thumb of his right hand. That was the spot where his flesh had been torn by the tusk-like mandible of a nightmare from another world. The fingers still moved just fine, but the wound ached whenever the weather changed. Scar tissue was like that.

At least the physical scar tissue. The emotional kind was much worse.

He thought about the thing he'd fought. By all rights he should have died that day, same as the men in his command, but that had been a long time ago and much more a case of blind luck than strategy.

N N N

Claymore mines didn't care what they shredded, they just did their work. He'd seen the thing moving, charging for him, and had ducked just before the detonation.

Green fluorescent blood had been everywhere, but he didn't think he'd killed the bastard. He'd seen the way the leaves rustled as it ran away, and he'd followed the trail until it vanished in a small clearing.

Even if he'd been able to catch the thing, he wouldn't have gotten away with any trophies. The situation was too hot to let him carry a heavy burden. The single piece he'd grabbed had been part of a telescoping spear that was made of a lightweight and incredibly tough metal.

He had hard evidence.

N N N

Hard evidence was coming his way again.

He was thrilled.

And he was terrified.

It was one thing to know that something existed, and another completely to confront the physical proof after years of self-doubt. The voices, the murmurs, the often bold looks of contempt had all taken a toll on him. It had been decades since he'd seen an alien, and he wondered how much his mind had edited what he'd seen back then.

Had he imagined the size of the creature? Did he edit that size the way a fisherman changed the length of his biggest catch, or the one that got away?

Elliott could close his eyes and claim to still see the face of the nightmare, but what details did he remember clearly? The dreadlock-like appendages that fell from the head? Yes, he still remembered them. The eyes? Maybe. The mouth so like the mandibles of a spider? Or the fangs nearly hidden by those vile moving barbs?

He couldn't say for certain. The only time he thought he knew with any true conviction was when he was asleep, and the fucking thing came after him again. Of course those particular dreams seldom ended the same way as reality.

He sat at his desk for a long while, resting his head in his hands and breathing, doing his best to focus on the work ahead. There would be cataloging of equipment, and there would be so many pictures to take, proof of the creature's existence. And then if he had his way, there would be an autopsy or, better still, a vivisection. So much more could be learned from a living creature.

The Reapers wouldn't be back for at least two hours.

That little voice in his head, the one he did his best to ignore, reminded him that he still had time. He didn't want to listen, but the voice was insistent, and try though he might, he could not make it grow silent. In time he gave in.

Just one little drink. A nip to calm the nerves that wanted to make his hands shake uncontrollably. What could it hurt?

One little drink.

He didn't take a fast snort. He savored the liquor. If he

didn't take his own sweet time he'd blow back half the bottle and never blink. That couldn't happen—not now. Not when he was so damned close to vindication.

N N N

The day after they got reamed out by the general, Elliott and his men went deep into the jungle. There was little they could actually see, little proof that anything was happening in those woods, but there was enough.

Fowler was a long-time hunter who knew how to look for tracks. He was surprisingly good at it, too. There weren't a lot of marks to prove that anything had gone that way. A few branches bent against the direction of certain trees. An occasional mark. The most telling ones were the muddy prints on a few of the branches, several feet off the ground. Once Fowler realized the bastard was moving through the trees, tracking him became much easier.

The heat was stifling and the sweat ran down Elliott's face, ignoring the brim of his hat that should have captured it, and dripping down to sting his eyes to the point of tears. That, and the damned bugs. Nowhere he had ever been was as teeming with insect life as Vietnam.

They stalked their killer as carefully as they could. They were spooks, and they'd earned the name well enough, not only because they were creepy to the average GI—he knew how the soldiers felt about them—but because they dealt with shit that no one wanted to think about, and they trained the locals in new ways to hunt and deal with their enemies.

All of which meant nothing.

It was one thing to know how to torture or terrify an enemy. It was something else entirely to deal with an alien that hunted them like animals.

They thought they were prepared. They were wrong.

✕ ✕ ✕

Woodhurst heard the news and smiled. He'd be heading back to the Stargazer base just as soon as he could, but in the meantime the news was good for a change. He and Traeger met for lunch and he filled the CIA man in on the latest.

"Sounds like getting funding should be a cakewalk now, General."

Traeger was smarmy. He still didn't like the man, but it looked like he was helping turn the tide almost as much as the news would. Two of his contacts had already said Traeger was making solid steps forward on procuring the finances that Stargazer needed, and if that meant Woodhurst had to put up with the man, well, it was a small price to pay.

"I never trust funding until I see the check, Will," the general said, "but it's a step in the right direction, and I'm already hearing tales of your work. Thank you in advance. Even if nothing comes of it, I appreciate the backup."

"We're all on the same team here, General," Traeger replied. "We all want the same things. Now, maybe, it looks like we're getting what we want." That smile again. "We got the prize, but how're the Reapers holding up?"

"That's the rough part." Woodhurst frowned. "Three dead and one who's lost an arm."

Traeger frowned. "That's a steep price."

"What else could we do? They're the best-trained soldiers I've ever dealt with, and we've seen what they can do in almost any circumstances—but this? Entire teams were taken out in LA during the last encounter. When you get down to brass tacks, we're lucky the casualties were so low." Knowing the truth of those words didn't take the sting out of them in the least. The Reapers were a cohesive unit, and half of them had just been removed from the picture.

"Maybe we can work out a new team or two with a bigger budget," Traeger said. "We play this the right way, we'll have enough to make sure the Reapers never suffer that sort of casualty again."

"I'd like that, but I'll settle for enough to get the work done without having to spend half my days doing a song and dance up here."

Traeger smiled thinly and nodded. "I think we can guarantee that now, General. I truly do." He looked down at his bowl of clam chowder. "We get a few pictures, just a few to tease the right people, and we can write our own checks. I believe that."

Woodhurst nodded his head. "I think I can arrange something. Just need to make sure we have a secure server to send the information."

"Good. That's good," Traeger replied. "By this time tomorrow we'll have all the information we need to head back home, General. I think we're going to rock this town to its foundations, and when we're done we're going to make sure the USA is once again the only super power that matters."

Woodhurst smiled. That was one thing on which they agreed. The Russians, the Chinese, and all the lesser powers and wannabes were in for a very big surprise in the near future. Of course, first they had to get there.

Woodhurst smiled his thanks as the waitress brought his porterhouse steak. He'd regret it later but just now he felt like a little celebration. A very small one. Nothing was written in stone yet, and three very good men were dead because they had followed his orders.

They were dead, but they'd gotten the job done.

For the first time in US history, a predatory alien species that hunted humans had been successfully captured. Soon they would glean the information they needed about the creature and its technology. Somewhere out there was a ship that had brought the creature across light years of space and managed to hide so completely that every satellite in orbit around the planet failed to catch so much as a heat trail.

That sort of technology was the exact sort of thing that would change the face of global politics. He intended to make certain the change was for the better.

14

Sean Keyes and Roger Elliott stood together in the decontamination chamber, both in their birthday suits and meticulously looking at spots on the wall rather than each other.

"You nervous about this, Commander?" Keyes didn't just look like his father, he had the same mannerisms, if slightly less intense. The difference, of course, was that his father had been a Company man, and Keyes himself was a medical specialist with a serious background in xenobiology and both reptilian and arachnid physiology.

He'd read the notes when he was in school. Anyone else would have been told that there were no notes to read, but Elliott himself had made the decision to break the rules and let the college frat boy look at the long series of observations his father had written before he died at the hands of an alien hunter.

That was something they had in common. They'd lost important people in their lives to the things that hunted humans for sport, or maybe to prove that they were adults in their society. It was hard to say with any certainty.

Elliott looked at him and gave a weak smile. "Nervous? No. Terrified. Excited. Angry, maybe, but not so much nervous." He shook his head and closed his eyes as the light in the room intensified and burned away a fine layer of anything that was touching his body, including skin and hair.

"No? Hell, I'm nervous," Keyes responded. "Excited, too. I mean, I've been studying these things for as long as I've been able to. And now, finally, I get to see one."

"That's the difference, maybe. I've seen one before." Elliott tried not to think about it. The thoughts came just the same, echoing through his mind and every fiber of his being.

Keyes stared at him, speaking carefully, doing his best to keep his face neutral. Elliott remembered the man's father, how he did the same sort of thing, and found himself wondering how close they'd been. Was it genetics that made him respond like that? Or was it nurture?

"You know, I've got a full run of tests ready," Keyes said. "Blood samples, saliva, skin, hell, even stool samples—the very best we could muster on our budget, and that's really a lot. I know you're the reason for that, too. I know you called in a lot of favors just to get me the DNA sequencer." The kid smiled nervously and licked his lips.

"I've got just about everything I could possibly need to identify everything I can, right here," he continued, practically babbling. "I've got ultrasound, I've got an MRI machine. I have enough shit to analyze this creature a hundred different ways. Hell, as you well know I have everything I need to cut that thing apart and damn near put it back together again. And even with all of that, I don't know if I have enough."

Elliott nodded. "I know what you mean. I've wanted to see what makes one of these things tick for as long as I can remember, hell, just about since I needed to shave."

"It's never happened before in human history, Pappy. We're going to examine an otherworldly life form. We're going to see what its capabilities are. What sort of life it is, and how it can survive here." There was almost a reverence in his voice, and Elliott shook his head.

"You seem remarkably well balanced for a man whose father was killed by one of these things."

Keyes looked at him for a moment with an intense stare, and Pappy started to apologize. Sometimes he forgot himself.

Then Keyes smiled. It wasn't a kind expression.

"Don't mistake enthusiasm for acceptance, Pappy. I want this sonofabitch for a reason. I know what it did. I've looked at the pictures. I know exactly how my daddy died."

"I'm sorry, Sean, I didn't mean—"

"No, it's all right. I get it," he said. "You just have to understand, I intend to learn everything I can about this thing. I'm going to do every test I could possibly need to do, and then I'm going to do some special tests. I figure they're tests you might be interested in, too."

"Yeah?"

"You ever see what happens when you excite a pleasure receptor?" Keyes smiled. "I mean excite it with a live electrode, of course. I intend to find out exactly what this thing's thresholds are, especially for pain, Pappy. I intend to test that threshold roughly a hundred times at the very least. For accuracy's sake, you understand. In the name of science." His eyes glittered. "I'll do everything by the book. Hell, Pappy, you damn near wrote the book in this case. I'm just going to add a few hundred footnotes."

Pappy smiled as he slipped into his hazmat outfit.

"Gotta go, Pappy. We're expecting a very important guest." He spoke even as he was sliding a surgical mask over his face. A moment later he was securing the airtight seals on his own suit.

Elliott nodded and watched the younger man moving away from him and toward the guest they had both been waiting for. He wasn't alone in his hatred of the alien. He also wasn't alone in his desire to see the damned thing suffer, but priorities were priorities. He would have to take care of information before he could take care of vengeance.

Sometimes it was good to know you weren't alone in the universe, even if that same knowledge was the source of most of your fears.

15

The Reapers carried their prize off of the copter and put it onto the gurney that was waiting for them. There were more gurneys as well, but this one was reinforced and required the combined strength of three men to move it on a steady course.

The move was uneventful, primarily because the alien seemed to be in a chemically induced stupor. Just to be safe they kept it bound tightly at the wrists and ankles.

Five minutes after arriving at Stargazer the Reapers surrendered their charge to the tech team headed by Sean Keyes. He was wearing a biohazard outfit and a surgical mask under the faceplate. The man smiled, or at least his eyes did behind the surgical mask, but it wasn't a sign of happiness so much as a grimace when he studied the shape.

"He's a big one, isn't he?"

Tomlin nodded. "It's been tranked. It's bound. It's breathing." He paused, then added, "It killed three of my men—Strand died en route—and we've got a fourth who might not make it. Don't take any chances."

"Preaching to the choir, Tomlin."

Tomlin understood. Sean Keyes was a second-generation alien hunter. His father had been killed in Los Angeles while trying to capture one of the things.

"Sorry," he said. "I just don't want anyone else getting hurt."

"I'll be very careful." Tomlin nodded again and then moved back to the other gurneys. Three of them sported body bags. The fourth held Burke, who was unconscious, breathing rapidly, and as white as a gallon of whole milk. His arm was gone, cut away by the alien.

Keyes called after him. "Get yourself to quarantine straight away. No playing. I mean it."

"Quarantine? What for? That thing's still got a mask on."

"It's also been bleeding all over the place, and we can't take any chances on biohazards."

Tomlin frowned.

"You ever see *War of the Worlds*?" Hill asked.

Keyes shook his head. "You want to kill everyone off with a virus you caught from this thing? Go to quarantine. Now. I won't be far behind you."

"What about the cops?" Tomlin demanded.

"We've got a team in there. They'll be taken care of—the drug dealers, too." He smiled grimly. "It'll be complicated. Funny thing, though, what happens when a meth lab explodes."

Tomlin still didn't feel like going into isolation.

"Go on," Keyes continued as gently as he could. "We've got Burke. We'll do everything we can."

Hill looked at him and shook his head. There wasn't much chance the poor bastard would survive. The blood loss alone was catastrophic. They'd taken turns trying to stave off the worst of the blood flow, but it had taken time and they were all exhausted.

Four medics appeared and grabbed the gurney sporting Burke. They moved away as fast as they could walk.

"Fuck." It was all he could think to say.

Hill nodded and then pointed. "Get on down to the medical station. You took a few hits."

"I'm not the one with a scalp wound. Get yourself down there."

Hill looked hard at him. "We'll go together." Tomlin didn't have the energy to argue, so he walked alongside his second in command.

N N N

Pappy Elliott found them a few minutes after they had settled in for their examinations. He was wearing a biohazard suit as well. The Reapers sat on adjoining tables, and each of them had a pair of medics looking after them. Two of the doctors posted at the facility were busy with Burke, doing what they could for him.

"Gentlemen, when you are done here," Elliott said, looking at the Reapers and the medics, "you will *all* report to quarantine." They looked back, understanding where he was coming from. He'd been in their situation once, and had lost men to the exact same source. They were connected now, part of a very small community of survivors.

It felt nothing at all like a badge of honor.

"You did good, boys. I'm proud of you." It wasn't much, but it was enough. Mostly Pappy didn't offer praise as much as he offered advice. A moment later he was on his way and they knew where he was going. They'd already faced the enemy, but for Pappy it hadn't happened yet. He'd been looking forward to staring at this particular demon for a very long time.

Tomlin felt the fear come back, felt grief try to reach out from his center and wrap thorny vines across his insides, and he forced those emotions back.

"What the fuck is that thing?" he said the words to himself, but he said them aloud, and Hill answered.

"That is a predator, pure and simple," he said. "That thing is a hunter, and it came here on a fucking safari to catch big game. It's after trophies."

"How many did it kill?"

"At least ten cops. A few of the people the cops were there to get. Three of us. Four, I guess. Damn thing barely got a scratch on it 'til we got there." Hill shook his head and rolled his eyes when the medic working on him pushed his head forward to get a clear look at the wound.

"Just stay still, my friend," the man said, "and you'll be stitched in no time." He administered an injection of painkillers. Hill gritted his teeth and he waited. Every muscle was tight.

The medic continued, "Listen, you need to take it easy. Seriously. You took a bad hit and there's a possibility of a concussion. You need to look out for…"

Hill tuned the rest out. The painkillers had taken effect, and when the medic got to work all he felt was an odd tugging sensation. If he'd felt more than that, Tomlin was fairly certain the medic would have been spitting teeth all over the floor. As it was, Hill's lips moved with each pull of the thread. He was counting the stitches.

"What do they call predators at the top of the food chain?" Tomlin's question caught him off guard.

"Apex," Hill replied. "They call them apex predators."

"That thing better be the apex," Tomlin growled. "I don't want to see what might be able to take those bastards on."

Hill looked his way and bared his teeth. "We took the fucker on. We would have killed it, too, but we were told to take it alive. We had our fucking hands tied, Tomlin. If we'd been using lethal force, there'd be more of us still alive."

"Not again." Tomlin shook his head. "We delivered one live specimen. We ever go against one of those things again, I intend to bring it down with extreme prejudice."

"Amen to that, brother." Hill stared at the distant wall and counted silently as the medic kept sewing his flesh back together. After a moment he said, "Four of us gone. Half of us. All because they wanted to study that thing." He frowned. "Wonder what they have in store for it."

"Orologas would have said it was important to better understand their language."

Hill snorted. "King would have agreed. Poor bastard finally got religion today, and wouldn't you know it, his god killed him in a second flat."

"Well, at least he got confirmation before he went."

"Yeah. Amen to that, I guess."

They grew silent then, both lost in their own thoughts

as the medics finished making sure they were still intact. Despite Tomlin's fears, Hill was fine—aside from the stitching. Bastard had too hard a head to get a concussion.

Just ten minutes after they'd arrived, the medics and the Reapers alike were sent into decontamination, where the outer layer of their skin and a few millimeters of hair got burned away before they were shoved into cells behind a heavy glass wall. They had toilets, televisions, laptops and recycled air, and would remain in that area for at least the next three days, if all went according to plan. Better to make sure they weren't going to spread a goddamned space plague, he supposed.

✄ ✄ ✄

Elliott looked at the creature and remembered how to be afraid. He stood before it with no armor and no weapons. Instead he wore a hazmat suit and his skin tingled from the layer that had been burned away.

The first few people who'd encountered the creature, including the Reapers, were locked into confinement for at least the next seventy-two hours. If any signs of contagion showed up, they'd be locked away for longer.

When he saw the first video footage of the room where they had the creature, it felt like he'd damned near had a stroke. There were scientists and medical doctors with it, and only one of them had considered the risk of infection. It was a goddamned breach of protocol.

He understood though. On the one hand this was an amazing opportunity. On the other, they'd prepped for this, planned for this, and considered the possibilities for months on end. The Reapers could be forgiven, and the first responders, as well, but aside from them there was no excuse for the sort of sloppiness he'd seen in action.

His throat was still sore from the reaming he'd administered to the people in charge of the area. They'd been taken away, and the entire area had been scrubbed before any further work could be done. Now the beast was in a sealed laboratory and it was sedated. That was the way it was supposed to be handled.

They had removed the armor, and removed the mask that covered its face. It was worse than he'd remembered. Somewhere along the way he'd forgotten the texture of the thing, or how its head where the dreadlocks fell had reminded him of a crab's exoskeleton. The mottled colors of this one were different. The dark spots were similar, but he remembered the thing having more of a greenish hue.

He thought all of that while he looked at the creature and felt his skin break into a sweat. Elliott licked at his lips and felt his breath tremble as he exhaled. How the hell could he have forgotten so many fine details?

Well, really, that was part of the job, wasn't it? If he couldn't forget things, he'd have never survived being part of the Phoenix Program in the first place. He did things in Vietnam that were dubiously legal and morally checkered. He was hardly in a place where he could be expected to remember every detail.

Even though the thing was already unconscious, it was properly restrained. He made certain of that. The restraints were thick leather and stainless steel, and heavy enough to stop a rhino from pulling free, according to what he'd been told. The links certainly looked as if they'd stop any attempt to break them.

Ignoring the walking nightmares for a second, Elliott reached over and picked up the war mask. The interior was scuffed and worn. The exterior showed signs of previous conflicts—several deep scratches including one gouge that was very fresh, and looked like a bullet mark. He pulled out the digital camera he'd slipped into his pocket earlier and snapped several pictures of the mask, then of the two gauntlets. One had heavy blades still extended, and the other sported a security cover that protected the computer system he knew was there.

He didn't open it. He wasn't a science type. He'd leave it for them to examine when the time was right. Instead he set the piece down carefully and took a shot of the grisly bone-and-skull necklaces the thing had been wearing. Trophies—that's what they had to be. A couple of the skulls didn't even look like they belonged to anything on Planet Earth, and he made certain to take close-ups of those. He never knew, really, what a scientist might find important.

Elliott wasn't alone in the room. There were other people all around, a half-dozen of them, and they moved carefully. He figured that was to avoid catching his attention. They were worried about him.

They had every right to be worried. Elliott did his best to look innocuous, but to other people he was a scary man, even when he wasn't trying to be scary. Somewhere along the way he'd gotten too intense for most people to be comfortable around him. He knew it, he understood it, and if he'd really cared he probably could have gotten better at hiding it. The problem was, he didn't care enough. It wasn't worth the trouble of changing.

His wife had left him a long time ago, and there were no kids. Without those factors, it wasn't worth the effort. The Reapers weren't scared of him, and he would've kicked the asses of any who were.

He knew it happened to a lot of his kind: the "spooks." Maybe that helped them earn the name, because they looked and acted haunted. Not likely, but it made sense in its own way. Then again, not every operative had a personal demon that weighed in at four hundred pounds and stood over seven feet tall.

He took pictures of the feet, counting the toes. Seven per foot. One at the heel, one small nailed appendage at each side of the ankle, four toes at the front. He wondered if they'd all been bendable once. He'd seen several different birds in Vietnam that had been tamed and set on perches. They'd had four toes and they'd been able to perch with them, and grasp objects. The alien was wearing sandals. He took them off as gingerly as he could and took photos of the bottoms of the feet.

He was just taking pictures of the legs when the creature let out a small grunt.

Elliott didn't actually achieve escape velocity when he jumped back, but it wasn't for lack of trying. His heart hammered in his chest and his vision went gray for a second. He was too old for sudden scares, damn it.

The good news? The people around him had backed away just as quickly. It saved a little face.

Dr. Keyes came up to him and smiled.

"You're a better man than I am, Gunga Din."

"What do you mean?"

"I mean, I almost pissed myself."

That massive, inhuman head turned in their direction, and the eyes that had haunted Elliott's nights for as long as he could remember focused on Keyes.

"It's awake." Elliott barely recognized his own voice.

The creature turned its gaze, examining him with cold detachment. That vile mouth moved, and the teeth showed clearly. Along the right side of the face several thick scars showed where something with claws had left substantial wounds, once upon a time. Along the brow and closer to the dreadlocks there were spines that grew from the thick skin, and where there were scars the spines were missing, marking the damage even more vividly.

Pappy Elliott stared, and the thing stared back, its gaze unreadable. How could anyone know what the damned things might think? They were too far removed from human in every reasonable sense.

"What the fuck are you looking at, you bastard?"

The creature narrowed its eyes, and then it made a sound that could only be one thing. It *laughed*. Like it knew what his words meant. Elliott felt his face flush red with an uneasy mix of embarrassment and anger.

"You laugh," he growled. "Go ahead. There's only one of us that's strapped down."

To make his point he leaned in, lifted the camera, and took a close-up of the creature's face. He made sure to clearly track the line of scar tissue and to show the eyes in all their unholy glory. The alien grew silent again and watched as he continued taking pictures of its head, the neck, the torso and the hands at the end of those bound wrists.

The thing did not struggle in its bonds. Instead it merely watched him.

He turned away.

"Only one of us."

The sound came from the thing strapped to the table. He could tell without a doubt, but when he turned back the alien's face was turned away from him.

Rage filled him, unbidden. Not fear—not now—just a boiling, seething fury that he could not express, not with so many witnesses.

Instead he took more pictures and carefully catalogued each item that they had taken from the thing. There were small discs that sprouted a half-dozen deadly curved barbs. There was the bloodied discus-like object that had cut one of the Reapers nearly in half. Orologas died as a result of the blade along the edge, and the weapon still had his blood dried onto it.

There were several metal drawers in the room, each with a separate lock. They could have easily used those to store each and every item the monster carried. Instead Elliott took the helmet, the discus, and the shoulder-mounted laser thing. While it watched, he moved all of those devices to a different place. There was a small vault two rooms away. All three items went into that vault and were sealed away. Not for security reasons, but more because he suspected those were the items the bastard would miss the most.

That gave him some small satisfaction.

As an afterthought he took the computerized gauntlet and put it in the same vault. He made sure to show the piece to his prisoner before taking it away.

It didn't make a sound.

16

Fowler was the one who found it. He remembered that clearly enough. The man was nearly quivering with excitement when they got close.

"Maybe half a click from us. These tracks are as fresh as they come." By that point Fowler was whispering, because they had no idea what they were up against, only that it was deadly in the extreme.

Suddenly there was a scream behind them. It was Simons, with a nearly perfect round hole driven through the back of his skull. Whatever had hit him, it punched through his head and into a tree he'd been leaning against for a moment. It was a damned bad way to die and that was all there was to it.

Simons had been at the back of the group, yes, but he was plainly visible to Eppinger and Groff. They heard him scream and turned in time to see his head slammed against the tree. They'd watched while he died from an injury that appeared for no apparent reason. It wasn't a bullet wound. It wasn't an explosive. It was just a death blow that shouldn't have been possible.

Then things went sideways.

Eppinger and Groff sent a hail of lead, tearing the hell out of the trees behind Simons's corpse. If anyone was back there they were dead before the firing was done. But when they checked, if there was anything at all that they had hit and killed, there was no physical evidence.

Fowler scanned the area as carefully as he could.

"There," he hissed. "Up in the trees."

By the time Elliott looked, there was nothing to see.

"What was it?"

"I don't know," Fowler admitted. "Just movement—I couldn't get a good look."

They kept looking. There was nothing else to do about it. They grabbed the dog tags, wrapped Simons up in a canvas sack. The body had to be left behind, though. If they could, they'd pick it up on the way back, but there was no telling when that would be. They had every intention of continuing their march until they found what they were looking for.

Elliott said a prayer for the man.

⋆ ⋆ ⋆

His faith was tested for the next two days.

Groff disappeared. They never found an indication of what happened to him. No body, no tags. Not even a drop of blood. It was always possible that he just decided to run, but Elliott didn't believe it for a second.

A few hours later they found Eppinger, or at least most

of him. Something had literally torn his skull and spine free of his body. The remains were close by, yet he'd never made a sound. That was the most terrifying part. The poor bastard went off to relieve himself—his pants were still down around his ankles when they found him—and something killed him and pulled him in half without making enough noise to alert the men standing maybe thirty yards away.

N N N

The third day saw Carter skinned. The man had several tattoos that he'd gotten abroad. Morbidly Elliott wondered if that was why his flesh was peeled away.

On the fourth day Elliott, Rabinowitz, Fowler, Hancock, Burton, and Chambers were all alive and well when the sun went down. Before they settled for the night Fowler moved away from the group and laid out some Claymore mines. He made good and damned sure that everyone knew where to look and where to not go. They'd lost enough people to whoever was hunting them.

Claymores were simple and direct. Fowler pointed them in the direction he wanted covered, laid out the tripwire, and whatever triggered the damned thing would get enough buckshot to shred a squadron of soldiers. Fowler had set them up the last two nights and never caught anything, but he remained persistent when Elliott would have given up.

The first explosion woke them up.

"What the fuck was that?" Burton said, keeping his voice low.

"The Claymores," Fowler replied, a hint of victory in his voice.

The second detonation saw them ready for whatever was coming their way. Except there was no way they could prepare for what they saw.

The enemy crouched in the branches above. It looked to be at least seven feet in height, big and muscular, with a metal mask over its face and weird hair like dreadlocks. It wore armor on its shins, knees, and part of the thighs. There was some sort of contraption on its shoulder, and it was bleeding in a dozen or more places. The blood was green.

It was bloodied, and it was pissed.

The thing dropped down from a height of easily twenty feet, and when it dropped it swept a heavy blade in front of it and cut Chambers in half. The guy never had a chance. He was hacked in two, and Elliott was the first among them to scream bloody murder at the sight.

Fowler came up with a hunting knife in one hand and his pistol in the other. He took a stab with the knife—a wicked thing with a seven-inch blade—and caught the creature as it was charging toward him. Then he fired the gun, once, and the bullet bounced off the armor on the creature's chest.

A second later Fowler exploded.

The device on the thing's shoulder was a mounted weapon, and it blew him apart.

Hancock lifted his M-16 and fired it repeatedly at the thing, hitting it several times. He had much the same luck as Fowler, though, and most of the rounds struck armor and were deflected. Two hit flesh and cut through it, but the monster didn't stop. It fired something from a wrist mount and Hancock fell back with a smoking wound in his chest. He coughed blood before he stopped moving.

Rabinowitz and Burton ducked into the trees and tried to flank the thing, and that left Elliott in the thick of it. The beast came for him; he saw the blades pop free from the wrist gauntlet, and managed to block the first attack. They came in fast and he stepped in closer, rather than dodging, and used both of his arms to stop the blow, but his best was barely enough.

The thing grunted and flexed and the next thing he knew he was hurled through the air and rolling into the foliage. He came to a stop with his heart hammering away and his eyes bugged out, not just because his opponent was so damned big, but also because he was inches away from the tripwire for one of Fowler's Claymores.

Before it could come for him again, Rabinowitz moved around from behind a tree and fired several rounds. The line of holes spread upward from the left thigh and into the stomach of the creature. Three more blew into the massive body, each of them leaking a vile green blood that shouldn't have been possible. He understood then that the thing had to be from another planet, or another dimension, or damned near *anywhere* that wasn't Planet Earth.

Even as that thought came to him, Rabinowitz's round found the face of the creature—the metal mask that hid that face away, at least—and blew a hole through its eye socket. The head snapped back for a moment, and then another jet of the foul green blood spilled out.

The roar that came from the thing made his guts tighten and his teeth clench. The thing fell back and screeched and then moved quickly around one of the trees.

Elliott should have fired on it while he had the chance. Even though he was still on the ground, it was in his line of sight. But instead he froze, mesmerized as the alien took off its face mask and looked around. It was as ugly as anything he'd ever seen, and it was royally pissed off.

Alien? Demon? Whatever the damned thing was, it was the stuff of nightmares. One eye was missing, but the other glared balefully as it scanned around, searching for the source of its pain. It disregarded a wound that would have sent an ordinary man into shock.

The creature saw Rabinowitz and flung something through the air. The man tried to dodge, but failed. An instant later he was on the ground and screaming. Half of his arm was gone, and his M-16 lay next to him.

There was a chance Elliott could still save Rabinowitz, but whatever had struck him came back around and took off the top of the poor bastard's head.

The creature came for him.

Lying as he was on the ground and looking at the monster charging his way, time slowed to a crawl. Elliott seemed to have all the time in the world to take in the details of the creature. The head of the thing, the face of the beast with its blown-out eye and tusks and a mouth full of fangs and mandibles that opened like some twisted, deadly flower.

He rolled away from the Claymore mine and started to

stand, and still it moved in his direction. Reaching for his pistol, he felt the grip, caught it in his fingers and pulled it free, aiming with his mind more than his eyes. His eyes were only for the thing careening his way.

He was a dead man and he knew it.

But he would take the thing with him when he went.

His shot was true. The bullet hit his target in the bared part of the torso and punched a hole big enough to toss a lime through. Still it came, roaring as it pulled out a stick that expanded into something larger. He fired again and missed. The creature dodged to the side even as he pulled the trigger.

It thrust the spear at him and Elliott held his hand out as if that might somehow stop the thing. It did not. The tip smashed into his ribs and skidded across bone with a lightning bolt of pain. And then it was on him.

The spear was gone and the creature lifted him off the ground, one massive, hot, clawed hand on either side of his ribs. His blood ran along its left hand and drizzled down its forearm as it hefted him as easily as a parent lifts a toddler. He kicked at the thing and did no damage, then swung his hand at the nightmare face. One of the tusks punched into and through the web between his forefinger and thumb. The blade-like teeth beneath it were a hair's breadth from his fingertips.

It pulled back and roared in his face, that one good eye burning with hatred. His other hand still held the pistol, and he aimed and fired—again without giving any thought. From two feet away he managed to miss. It shouldn't have been possible.

Heavy claws scraped past his sweat-stained uniform and carved into his sides. Elliott fired again even as the creature threw him backward.

While Elliott was free-falling through the air, Burton shot the bastard four times in the back. It staggered and turned, the mounted weapon spinning and aiming for the man even as the blood pumped furiously from its wounds. The cannon did its business and Burton died in a flurry of brilliant lights that blasted through his flesh and took him apart.

Bloodied, perhaps even dying, the goddamned nightmare came for him again, screeching and warbling and eager to tear him apart. Managing somehow to stand, Elliott spotted the tripwire and moved over it carefully. He saw the Claymore, knew where it was pointed. He also knew that with just one step he could be out of the cone of effect.

He took two, to be safe.

As the thing came closer he leaned down and hit the tripwire with the butt end of his pistol.

The explosion was so much more powerful than he'd expected. He knew there would be damage to the trees. He knew there would be noise. In that moment, however, it was greater even than the hellish thing that was reaching for him. The pellets locked inside the mine escaped at the speed of sound and blew through his assailant. Elliott saw the ripple of flesh, of the odd tentacle things on its head, as the body was shoved backward by the concussive force.

Pain exploded in his calf.

He hadn't gone *quite* far enough.

When he could think again—and he wasn't exactly certain how long that had taken—Elliott examined the wounds in his calf. They were minor. His boots had absorbed the brunt of the force, though he had no doubt he'd have been destroyed by the explosion if he'd been in the direct path. Looking around, he saw a spill of fluorescent blood that spread over a dozen feet in any direction.

The damned thing had to be dead.

It *had* to be.

Two hours of searching proved him wrong. There was a long trail of the stuff that ran from the area and moved hard toward the north. Following it, he kept track of his path. He couldn't afford to get lost in the woods, and he surely couldn't afford to lose the bodies of his men.

There was a strange sound, and he picked up the pace as best he could. The trail of blood led to a new wonder— an aircraft the likes of which he had never seen before. He had a cheap camera on his hip, and managed to snap a couple of pictures before the ship lifted straight into the air. The sound wasn't as loud as he expected it to be, though he had to protect his eyes from the debris it kicked up, and then it launched toward the sky.

He watched it vanish and tried very hard to tell himself it was all a fever dream.

N N N

But it hadn't been. It had taken most of his life, yet here he was and there the nightmare lay, bound and soon to reveal its secrets.

A lot of very good men had died for this to happen.

Elliott intended to remember all of them, and to make sure they were properly honored.

✦ ✦ ✦

The creature was angry with him. He had never seen it before, but it spoke to him and cast angry looks his way even as it went about scanning him with its primitive, boxy device.

The Yautja—the name for his people—seldom cared what others thought of them. Still, he was fascinated by the gray-haired individual's anger. Was it because of the prey he had already killed? Or had it encountered the Yautja before? There had been incidents over the years. He himself had hunted these things in the past, but he'd made certain not to leave survivors.

There was always a chance that previous hunters had been here, and not returned. That was part of what made hunting a challenge. If there was no danger, there was no honor to it. There was no glory for striking down creatures that could not defend themselves or could not hunt just as well, regardless of their level of technology.

More than once his chieftain had said that the technology of the Yautja came at least partially from adapting what they had found on other worlds, when the hunters discovered creatures that were more advanced in one way or another. There were precautions in place for protecting the technology they used. Their ships were hidden when they traveled, and when they landed their craft were locked and secured. The weapons were coded to the individual hunter. The key was kept in the control gauntlet.

He didn't know the faces of these creatures sufficiently to read them, but he trusted his instincts well enough to believe the gray hair was taunting him. It may have harbored an unresolved vendetta, or it might have been unsettled at encountering life from another world. Though the species possessed some capabilities in stellar travel, they were extremely limited.

In any event, he had only to wait. The gray hair was not done with him, and when it came back he would see how he could use that unexplained anger or fear to his advantage. If he could get past his restraints, the rest would be easy.

Let the weapons be taken. Even the control gauntlet. No one was foolish enough to leave without redundancies. If he could reach his ship he could track every item that had been taken from him, and he could either deactivate them remotely or set the self-destruct to eliminate the problem—along with the entire facility that held it.

He had always been a patient hunter.

17

Elliott stared at the bodies for a long time. He memorized their faces and reconciled the corpses with the young men he'd trained.

That was his responsibility. That was the cost he had to pay for being in charge of an elite team and sending them to their deaths. In time he would write the letters of condolence to any family, and he would make certain that the cause of death was listed as part of the ongoing skirmishes in the Middle East. That was one of the few advantages to having a war going on as far as he was concerned. There were plenty of politicians who might have pointed out the monetary benefits, but he wasn't a bureaucrat. He was a covert operative who trained others to handle shadow work.

He'd been "Pappy" to those boys, those deceased men who'd come up against a nightmare and failed to survive. He was the man who was supposed to keep them alive and well while they fought his demons.

In that, he was a failure.

There was success to crow about, yes. They'd caught the damned thing and now, hopefully, they'd learn enough to justify the expense both in money and in lives. With the technology they'd taken they could very likely find a way to locate the ship it had landed in, and then they'd have struck the mother lode when it came to technological superiority.

None of that made the need for a drink any less overwhelming.

No. Not a drink. He wanted to get ripped. His mouth watered at the notion of tipping back a bottle of tequila, or getting in a few serious snorts of vodka, gin, or Scotch. He knew he needed to stay away from the booze, but it called just the same and promised to ease away all of the anxiety in his guts and the doubts in his brain. It always made the same promises and he did his best to ignore them, because he knew in his soul that they were, in fact, lies.

Still, he salivated at the thought, and his left eyelid twitched just enough to make him grind his teeth.

The alien was one demon. The thirst was another. He needed to keep both of them in check, especially if he was going to accomplish everything he knew Woodhurst expected from him. But every damned time he closed his eyes, he could see that thing looking at him, and he could feel the guilt trying to wrestle its way into his mind over the deaths of four boys young enough to be his grandkids, if he *had* any grandkids. They were dead because somewhere along the way it became more important to capture that thing alive than to teach them how to survive against weapons that broke all the rules.

With an effort he pushed those thoughts aside and then peered at the pictures on his computer screen. The images were clear, not the least bit blurry, and Pappy shook his head, overwhelmed by the knowledge that *this* was hard evidence. This was vindication for decades of doubt and ridicule.

Woodhurst would be pleased.

That had to be enough for now.

He uploaded the files to the secure server and sent them to both Woodhurst and Traeger. Not all of the images, of course. Three pictures of the alien, four more of its devices. The rest would wait for later, but for the moment these would do the trick. They would make the point for any doubters.

When he was finished he looked at the autopsy shots of his boys. Those he would not send on. There was no need. There was nothing all that unusual about a dead soldier, after all.

"Enough, old man," he growled. "Stop being a whining little bitch."

He opened a new file on the computer, a Word document. A quick note and the address was in the right spot. Another look at the paperwork and the names were just so.

Dear Mr. and Mrs. Strand,

It is with profound regret that I must inform you of the passing of your son, Elmore.

I have had the pleasure of working with Elmore for the last two years. As the commander in charge of his unit I did my best to make certain he was prepared for any situation.

This Thursday, October 27th at 16:47 hours, Elmore had the misfortune of encountering several hostiles intent on attacking the installation where we both work and live. The attack was unexpected, as terrorist attacks most often are, and the sad fact is that Elmore was at the western gate when the hostiles attacked there, using several explosive devices in an attempt to breach security and proceed with the intent to kill as many innocents as they could.

Witnesses to Elmore's bravery are numerous, but Corporal Heath Duttweiller said it best, I believe, when he told me that if not for Elmore's bravery, the gates would have been breached and the entire facility would have been compromised.

I cannot possibly explain to you how very sad I am to have to write you this letter. I cannot hope to clarify the depth of my sorrow. Your son, Elmore, exemplified everything that a soldier should be. He was honest, he was brave, and his courageous actions saved the lives of every person at the base.

I have made recommendations that Sergeant Elmore Strand receive the highest possible honors for his bravery and sacrifice. I have never had the privilege of being a parent, but if I were and Elmore were my own son, I could not be prouder of all that he accomplished. Nor could I be more diminished by his passing from this world.

It was my honor to serve with Elmore, and to know him as well as I did.

You have my condolences and the gratitude of a grateful nation,

Sincerely,
General Douglas F. Woodhurst

That was one. Only three more to go. He would personalize each of them and send them to the general for his approval. Woodhurst was a busy man, and Elliott knew from conversations they'd had in the past that the man tended to procrastinate when it came to letters like these.

The boys didn't deserve to have their families kept waiting.

He finished the rest of the letters as quickly and carefully as he could, making certain to note the circumstances he created for each of their deaths. Then he shut down his computer, stood up, and headed for his quarters before he could do something stupid like reach for the flask he had locked in his desk.

ℵ ℵ ℵ

Traeger looked at the images and made hard copies. He would not risk carrying that sort of intel on his phone. That was the kind of thing that caused trouble down the line.

Pulling them out of the printer, he stared at each and every piece, fascinated and damned near ready to drool.

The alien creature was decidedly scary, and one look at that face confirmed what he'd already suspected—this thing was a predator. Anything with that many ugly-ass teeth and forward-facing eyes was guaranteed to be a carnivore. At least that was what he'd learned watching the National Geographic Channel.

Didn't explain sharks, but they were fish.

More importantly, there was proof of the technology. Not anything that couldn't be faked, of course, but there would have to be a little trust somewhere along the way. He had to trust that the people he spoke to would respect national security, and they had to trust that his evidence was genuine. Anyone who couldn't play by those rules was a waste of his breath.

While he was folding the pictures and sliding them into his jacket pocket, Woodhurst called.

"General," Traeger said, "I was just getting ready to call you." A lie, but a small one. At this point the man was a hindrance—but he could hardly say that.

"Will," Woodhurst said, "these images are positively astonishing." The man sounded excited. That was unsettling. Normally the closest he came to emotion was sounding disappointed in the world around him. Eeyore could be more cheery.

"I think it's going to make a difference, General," Traeger responded. "We're going to see big changes when it comes to financing the project." Both of them were careful not to voice any details. They had top-of-the-line cell phones, but even those would never be as secure as they wanted. That anyone could break the security coding was about as likely as a sparrow winging it to the moon and back, but why take chances?

"Just in time, I say," Woodhurst replied. "We needed a win, and we got one."

Traeger nodded and made sure to sound pleased. "A whole different world tomorrow, after our meetings. I don't think they're going to know what hit them."

"It's going to be a long day, Will. You get a decent night's sleep."

"I have a warm cup of milk and a shot of Scotch waiting to send me to dreamland," Traeger said. "I'm going to suggest the very same thing for you, General."

"Goodnight, Will."

"Goodnight, sir."

Sleep. Hell would freeze over first. He had four calls at the very least, and if he could make it happen there would be an equal number of short but necessary meetings before he went to bed. Politics could be a nightmare, no two ways about it—but some nightmares led to pleasant dreams. He just had to make sure his went that way.

Armed with his charm and a collection of amazing photos, Traeger left his room and prepared to change the world for the better.

N N N

Night settled over the Stargazer facility. Twice as many men as usual stood guard around a complex that only a handful of people even knew existed.

The stars came out and were half hidden by a deep humidity that marred the light and smothered details.

Those poor souls forced to stay outside in the night air did not perspire, they sweated. The air was thick and the heat of the day continued on into the night.

Inside the complex the people who had taken endless pictures of the newly captured alien saved the information they had gathered, speculated on what they would soon learn, and went for more coffee in the mess hall. There was no food permitted in the area where the alien hunter rested. Just entering the labs required hazmat suits and decontamination, per orders of Commander Elliott.

There had been a brief moment of sloppiness when everything happened at once, but it hadn't taken long for them to realize the risks of alien contagions, and just as importantly the risk that they might kill their prize with something as simple as a common cold. There was no way to know the immune system of an alien creature, though at this point blood and saliva samples had been collected and were being studied and cultivated.

As late as it was still the lab was a hive of activity, though everyone who came and went did so in silence, save for the soft beeping of the monitor strapped to the beast's chest and the occasional wheezing noises of the blood pressure cuff that strained on the alien's massive bicep. After a while, however, there was a lull in the activity. All of the samples were collected, and the researchers took them elsewhere to examine them well into the night. The lighting remained subdued, and four men constantly monitored cameras that were aimed at the creature. It appeared to be asleep, or in some other state of replenishment.

Pappy Elliott walked slowly, moving with surprising stealth for a man who swore to everyone that his joints were as creaky as an old ship on a stormy sea. He hadn't had a drink. God, he'd wanted to, but no. Not for this.

With his hazmat suit in place, he walked over to peer down at his enemy, his prize, his redemption, and he felt a deep loathing move slowly through him.

The mottled tone of the skin, the heavy brow, the frighteningly powerful body, all of it triggered him. Triggered—that was a word he understood better than most. For more than half of his life he'd been "triggered" by the notion of ever encountering a thing like this again, and here he stood.

His breath tried to fog the mask of his suit, but the cold air cycling from the oxygen tank compensated almost instantly. The view of his personal hell was not obscured.

He couldn't help it. He looked carefully at the slumbering demon's restraints and made absolutely certain that they were secured. They were.

The body wasn't completely bared, but it was close. The webbing that had covered the torso and legs was gone, very likely cut away, as the simple loincloth it wore was still in place. Simple? No, not really—it was made of hide of some kind, but it also had a belt, three pockets and a codpiece, for chrissake.

On a whim he checked the pockets and found nothing of interest but space lint. The guys who'd secured the thing to the table had long since taken care of whatever the thing kept there. Just as well.

He stared long and hard at that face. It wasn't the

creature he'd fought so many years ago—of course not. It was possible that the aliens had a way of regenerating an eye, but he hoped not. Besides, with the damage done by the mines back in the day, he still fostered a small hope that the creature died before it ever reached home. There hadn't been too many pieces left, when it was all said and done.

How far had this thing traveled? How long had it taken to move from another planet to this one? The garments it wore were distinctly primitive, but the technology it sported was a different story entirely.

Where did it come from? Did the species have an advanced society? There were no answers, of course. That was one of the reasons they'd wanted to capture it. But Elliott had other things he needed to know.

Why did they hunt? Was it for sport? Was it for prestige? Was there another reason they hadn't even begun to suspect? He had no way of knowing, but he *wanted* to know. It was a compulsion. It was more.

"Why do you do it? Hmm?" He spoke softly. "Why do you hunt people?" He didn't expect an answer, and wasn't even sure if he wanted to know if the thing could speak English. Elliott glanced at the closest table where, just under a layer of cloth, a large assortment of medical tools was kept. Vivisection. *It isn't just a job, it's an adventure.* Part of him wanted to grab one of the scalpels and start cutting. He resisted the urge, but it wasn't easy.

"What are you?" he asked, the words mumbled more than spoken. He moved slowly, carefully, studying the creature from every possible angle and avoiding the temptation to touch. Running his hands over the body, feeling the thing's heartbeat, would have made it too real. Hearing the heart monitor was bad enough. And if it was real, he might be tempted to destroy it.

Certainly it deserved to be destroyed. This creature and creatures just like it had killed an unknown number of humans—including four of his boys. Some of the reports they had, legends and lore as opposed to actual facts, mind you, came from a long ways back. Centuries.

"How long have you been coming to the planet? How long have your kind been hunting people?" It was impossible to know, yet what he did know—what he was certain of—was that they brought death wherever they went.

Elliott leaned in as close as he dared and stared long and hard. It wasn't a pretty face, not a handsome or noble face. It was the stuff of nightmares. He knew that for a fact. He had seen that face countless times over the years, when he tried to sleep.

The anger came back again and Elliott backed away. This would end, but it wouldn't end well, not if he stayed where he was.

The vast chest of the thing expanded in a deep breath and then exhaled in a long, slow sigh. The eyes fluttered behind closed lids.

Enough.

Elliott stepped further back and shook his head. Staying was only tempting fate, and he couldn't do that. Everything that the Company had worked for, everything that the general had worked for, everything that could potentially be learned by studying the monster in front of him, would go down the drain if he lost control of himself. No, personal satisfaction wasn't going to be the reason for his failure. He would have satisfaction in time. He had seen the creature brought down, and ultimately it would be killed. But first, they would learn all the secrets it had to offer.

He glanced again at the table full of medical instruments. There were any number of devices with which he could cause torture. But not today. Not now.

Turning, he walked slowly away from his target. Another time. Not today. Not with so much at stake.

A simple access code and the door opened. Another and it closed. In seconds a sliding wall of galvanized steel locked away the nightmares made flesh. Elliott nodded to himself and considered whether or not he could sleep. Maybe. Just perhaps.

He didn't look back.

✗ ✗ ✗

The gray hair left, and the portal shut with a *click*.

Without opening its eyes or showing any perceivable motion, the hunter used its thick claws against the animal-hide restraints. He knew he was observed and could not do anything that might raise an alarm.

18

Tomlin sat up on his medical cot and sighed, though it came out as more of a groan. Not ten feet away from him, Hill lay on the bed and stared at the ceiling. The man's face was set like stone and Tomlin left him in peace.

Sleep wasn't coming for him. His mind was too locked into an endless replay of everything that had happened, and he couldn't stop playing the "what if" game. What if he'd been faster? What if he'd made sure his people were better prepared? What if they'd followed the alien back to its ship, or nest, or whatever, and waited until the sun went down?

There was no good answer, of course.

"What if" was a game that could never be won. He could try until he was blue in the face, but he would never find a solution for what had already happened. Four of his people were dead. He'd been in charge when it happened. They caught the alien, but that meant nothing in comparison to the loss of life. Not to him, at least—not at that moment.

Burke died on the operating table. There was too much damage, too much blood loss, and not a damned thing they could do about it. Orologas, King, Strand… and now Burke.

Hill looked his way.

"It's shit."

Tomlin blinked. That Hill was even speaking was unexpected, but the words had no context.

"What?"

"You're thinking you could have done better, and maybe you could, but whatever you're putting yourself through? It's shit."

"What do you mean?"

Hill sat up, a stormy expression on his face. "Look, you know I'm watching your ass. I'm always watching your ass. You stand between me and what I want out of this gig, and I'd take you down so fast you'd scream if I thought there was a reason—but there ain't. You didn't do a damn thing wrong. So the games you're playing in your head? They're shit."

Tomlin looked away. He had to, because Hill's words struck closer to home than he cared to think about. He was torturing himself and he knew it, but Hill defending him was unexpected and enough to slip right past his resolve.

Hill remained silent behind him as he nodded rather than trying to speak.

"Thanks," he said finally. "I appreciate that."

"I was there, man. I saw the dead cops. I saw the dead everyone, and I saw that freaky bastard cutting down everything in sight. You did good—I couldn't have done any better."

They were silent for a while.

"I want it dead for what it did," Tomlin said. "Is that wrong?"

Hill snorted and shook his head. "No, man. I want it dead, too, but we had our orders and we followed them." Hill sighed and lay back down. "Tell you what, if we'd been using regular force instead of going for a capture, I think that thing would have gone down a lot sooner."

"I was thinking the same damn thing."

"Woodhurst gets back, we'll talk to him about that."

Tomlin nodded and then flopped back on his cot. His head hurt enough to distract from the grief that was trying to crush him.

"Hell of a thing." Hill leaned back on his forearms and once again stared at the ceiling. "That's all I can say. It's one hell of a thing."

There was nothing to add that they hadn't already said. They weren't friends, they were allies. More importantly, they were grieving.

They were quarantined. There was nothing else to do.

∦ ∦ ∦

He carefully looked around the sterile environment, making certain to keep as still as possible. There was not much to see. The creatures had turned down their artificial lighting, but his vision was more than adequate. Most of his equipment was missing. The Combistick was there, and two small cutting discs. His mask was gone, his armor was missing, both gauntlets were gone. The creatures had even taken his trophies to another room, likely for examination.

It would be a challenge breathing in the thin atmosphere for so long a time, but he would make do.

They had repaired him to the best of their limited abilities. His wounds had been cleaned and sewn. He could have cauterized them if he had retained his equipment. He understood now that the hunters that had taken him had been told to keep him alive. Otherwise he would be dead, a trophy for the victors.

The air was cold and artificially recycled. It had no scent. The silence in the room was nearly complete, so the only sound he could hear was the faint scraping of his claws working slowly and steadily on animal-hide restraints, and the sound of his own heartbeat made audible by the device attached to his chest.

He paused in his work when the automated door split open and once again a solitary figure entered. He did not know this one. The face was unfamiliar, locked as it was behind a glass visor and synthetic skin. It was not a warrior. Not a predator.

It moved closer, wheezing its synthesized air, and stood over him. It did not speak, but it looked at him carefully, examining his face, his head, his shoulders and torso, his arms. It did not touch, but instead it continued the slow and careful examination. Then unexpectedly, it spoke.

"I don't know what you are," it said. *"I don't care what you are. Mostly, you're an opportunity. I think we need that. I know Traeger needs that."* The words had a meter, and must have possessed meaning, though it was lost to him. The eyes scanned lower, stopping at the wrist, and he looked into the face of the pale blonde creature and did not move. The

bonds were almost severed, but underneath the surface, and he did not want to take any chances. He could break through now, he could kill the creature, but the doors would still be blocked.

Patience.

All hunters understood patience. All good hunters, at any rate. Satisfied with his wrists, the creature continued to examine him, studying his feet, looking at his legs and, once again, just as he thought he was safe, looking at his wrists. It said nothing but the expression on its face changed. The expression became sly. He understood in that moment that it knew. It understood what he was doing, and apparently it approved.

Unexpectedly the hand of the creature reached out and touched his with a familiar contempt. It was subtle, the sort of condescending notion a parent might offer a child who was not particularly bright.

He did not respond. Instead he simply stared. It spoke again.

"That's right, you go right ahead. Soon as you do, we will be on you. We have most of what we need for the moment. The Reapers are out of the picture, quarantined. Even if they want to, they can't get to you. You do what you have to. Either way, Traeger will approve."

Without an additional word, the pale-faced thing turned and headed for the exit. There was a panel with twelve buttons to the right of the door. Slowly, carefully, the hand of the creature moved to the panel. He could see what it was doing. He understood what it was doing. It did not offer a formal invitation, it merely offered access, a way out.

The door opened. Once more the thing turned and faced him. The bared teeth offered a feral sense of approval, and then it was gone, and the door was closing.

Slowly, carefully, he ran long claws over the leather bonds restraining his wrists. The world was silent. Cameras were watching; he was observed and he understood that. He also wondered how *well* he was being watched. When the first restraint parted, freeing his wrist, he made no expression. Moments later the second gave way.

He sat up quickly. The restraints at his ankles were easy to release. The wires attached to his chest and to his head came off easily and the machine that measured his pulse let out a sudden erratic noise.

Freedom was easy. He grasped the Combistick and it was a familiar weight in his hand, so that he let out a slight, soft, rattling sigh. His other hand captured the edged discs and slipped them into the pocket of his garb. One more grab and his sandals were once again his. They easily slipped into place.

The keypad beckoned. He used the same pattern he had seen the pale-faced creature enter, and was rewarded as the door opened. As yet there was no uproar.

This room was different. He had watched others come through, had seen the scan of eyes and hands and knew that he could not pass. Not as easily. The door was thinner, however—not as strong as the door behind him. It would take effort before he could get through. Once he did, however, he suspected an alarm would sound.

How long before they responded? How long before they could hope to stop him? Did they still want him alive?

Did they still need him breathing? They had examined him. They had taken many images and conducted tests.

Whatever they desired, he would have to move quickly once the door was open, and he would have to leave this place before anyone could stop him. This was a place of torture and pain. There were similar places on his own world and he had been to them on several occasions. His work required it. He would have treated anything new and unique in the very same way.

Had there been time, he would have looked for his weapons. He would have looked for his supplies. But there was no time.

As he had anticipated, the moment he forced the door open, changing the pressure in the room, the alarms started. He pushed past the opening and ran down the dimly lit hallway. He had been conscious when he was brought in and felt he could find his way.

Throughout the darkened corridors lights exploded into activity, changing night into day. Here and there additional lights flashed brightly. He ran as quickly as he dared, stalking through doors barely large enough to accommodate his height. A left, another left, a hard right, and there before him a rolling metal door. The very door they had brought him through in the beginning.

The klaxons were loud, disorienting, but not enough to slow his forward progression. His eyes did their best to adjust to the changes, but he had to admit he was limited without the special lenses contained in his mask.

He moved toward the door and was stopped by two of the native creatures coming from a nearby side door and drawing their weapons. The Combistick extended at the flick of his wrist and he drove the point through the head of his closest enemy.

The second of the creatures stopped and aimed, but hesitated when the blood of its companion spilled across its face. The Combistick was stuck in the skull of his enemy, so instead he lashed out with a foot and shattered the bones of the knee on the would-be assailant's leg. It cried out and fell back, firing a projectile into the ceiling in the process.

Striking a second time with his foot, he crushed his assailant's throat. There was no need for a third strike.

Pulling open the rolling metal door was easy enough, though the sound of it rumbling upward in its slot was disturbingly like thunder. The air outside was wet. Rain cascaded down from the sky in hard sheets and he moved out into the intensity of a growing storm.

A projectile struck behind him, and he turned to see who needed killing next. He recognized the features. It was the gray hair from earlier, the one that had spoken in challenging tones.

"*Stay where you are!*" The words meant nothing, but he recalled a few phrases from the past.

"No." The word felt strange in his throat.

Even as the gray hair took aim and let loose a shot, then another, the Combistick left his hand in a hard throw. The projectile hit his shoulder and carved a crease in his flesh, thankfully missing all bones and vitals. Nevertheless, it hurt.

The Combistick struck his enemy in the chest and sent

it staggering back from the open doorway and into the flashing lights of the broad corridor.

He could not go back for the weapon. Still, no hunter was the weapons he used. The hunter was the sum of the skills and heart he employed in seeking the kill.

Decision made, he nodded. Lightning exploded across the skies, and the clouds wept their frustration as he turned and ran.

N   N   N

Pappy Elliott saw the open door, saw the dead guards, and moved as quickly as he could. The alien was out there in the rain, larger than life and carrying one of its weapons. Ten feet, then twenty, then forty feet away from the open door. It moved so damned quickly, another fact he had forgotten over the years.

He fired a shot that narrowly missed the damned thing's head, and instead cut through the hide over its shoulder.

"Stay where you are!" he shouted.

It turned and looked in his direction, barked out something he couldn't quite hear past the torrential downpour, and then hurled something at him.

Back in Vietnam it was possible that Pappy might have avoided the spear. He certainly would have tried. All he could do now was stare at the damned thing as it ripped across the distance between them, and think that he should be moving his ass if he wanted to live.

He fired twice more at the thing standing out there in the rain, but couldn't tell if he hit it.

His traitorous old legs refused to move.

The gleaming spear struck true.

The pain slammed into his chest, blew through his heart and sent him flailing as his body smashed into the ground. He kept his grip on his service piece. That was something, he supposed, but at the end of the day, at the end of his life, it was hardly much of a victory.

The nightmare from his past watched as he fell, and then it nodded its head once, before moving out of his dimming field of vision.

19

Hill sat up as the alarms started blaring their warnings throughout the Stargazer compound. There was no doubt in his mind what was wrong.

"Motherfucker made a break for it," he gritted. "God *damn* it!"

Tomlin was already up and looking at the door of the isolation chamber. It was locked, of course. There were protocols to consider. Keeping everyone alive and safe from any possible contamination was a higher priority than letting any of the Reapers sneak out for a midnight snack.

The man's face pulled into a scowl of seething fury. He wanted out. He wanted another chance to deal with their alien prey.

Hill knew exactly how he felt.

Tomlin went over to the keypad on the door and tapped in his access code. Nothing happened. He tried three more times, his scowl growing more profound.

"It's no good," he said. "I tried overriding with my command status, but nothing."

Hill pushed past him and tried himself. He didn't doubt Tomlin, but sometimes you just had to see if you could do better.

ACCESS DENIED

Once, twice, and then a third time.

"Nothing." He knew the look on his face had to be close enough to Tomlin's to be scary.

Tomlin looked at the door. "Vacuum seal. No hinges. Stainless steel. We're screwed."

That was when the door opened.

They looked at each other, momentarily frozen with shock, and then headed for the opening, half expecting trouble for their efforts. Instead they found Jermaine Hyde and Kyle Pulver looking at them. Across the hallway the door to their room was already open.

"Turns out Hyde knows a lot about opening closed doors," Pulver said. Hyde remained silent. Hill nodded and looked to Tomlin.

"Let's go," the squad leader said. "Got some hunting to do."

"We limiting ourselves this time?"

When Hyde spoke it was almost unsettling. He seldom talked once they were engaged in business, and even when they were relaxing there was little he had to say.

Tomlin shook his head.

"We lost four. Not doing that again. We need to catch this thing before it gets away."

"Extreme prejudice time." Hyde actually smiled, an expression so rare that Hill felt a bit nervous. "Sweet."

Not far away a group of soldiers tore down the hallway, unconsciously moving in formation as they headed for what Hill assumed was the last place the predator had been seen. They headed in the opposite direction, moving into the Reapers quarters to grab their weapons and their armor.

It didn't take them long.

✗ ✗ ✗

Approaching the hangar door that led to the outside, they saw the medics trying to put Pappy Elliott back together. The Reapers could have saved them the time. He was too pale. His eyes were staring at nothing.

They exchanged looks that said all there was to say, really. They didn't have time to mourn his death. They'd get revenge for the man.

First, however, they needed to commandeer a vehicle.

✗ ✗ ✗

The chaos was nearly complete when Church picked up his phone and called Traeger. The connection was quick and Traeger answered on the second ring.

"What's up?"

"Someone left the birdcage open, and the bird has flown away."

"Better get our people on it."

"Already happening. No idea where it's gone, but we'll try to find it as quick as we can."

"Make it happen. I want it back before I get there, you hear?"

"You got it."

"Church?"

"Yeah?"

"Where's Pappy on all this?"

Church allowed himself a short, tight smile. "Sorry, I forgot to tell you. Looks like Pappy tried to stop the bird and got shit on."

"He alive?"

"There's a new opening for someone in charge of the Company's interests here."

There was a pause.

"What a pity," Traeger said. "What a mighty damn shame."

"Gotta go—there's a thing to catch up with."

"Make it happen." Traeger killed the connection.

Church stared at the wall for a moment and then sighed. It was going to be a long night. The agents under his command were already on the hunt for the alien. All he had to do was wait.

✗ ✗ ✗

Pappy's corpse was being lifted onto a gurney when Tomlin and the Reapers moved for the open door. There were several people in the way, some of them dressed for action and others standing around and trying to look like they were in charge.

The only people Tomlin answered to were Woodhurst and Pappy.

Pappy was dead and the general was out of town. When someone started speaking to him he ignored the voice and went out the open door into the rain. He didn't have to look back. He expected his men to follow and they did not disappoint him.

There was no clear sign of where the alien had gone, but he didn't need one. There was only one direction it would head in, unless the damned thing was addled. It would head for its ship, for supplies, and possibly even for home.

Going any other direction made no sense.

"I'm thinking south. You?" he asked Hill.

Hill nodded and that was enough. The four of them ran toward the closest available vehicle. They were in the garage. Finding one was easy.

Rank had its privileges. No one tried to stop them.

"Where exactly are we going?" Hyde settled in and started sorting through his equipment, even as Hill drove.

"South is all we have for now."

"Why south?"

"Everywhere it's left its mark is south of here, so it probably landed somewhere down there." Tomlin turned to address the two men in the back of the vehicle. Pulver was sliding into his flak vest, and Hyde continued to sort his weapons. Most of his equipment was hand-held and silent, which was exactly what the man preferred.

"What's the plan?" Pulver looked directly at him. "I just want to make sure we're all on the same side here."

Hill answered for him. "Motherfucker just killed four

of us. We caught it once and it killed *four* of us. We're not going to get a second chance to take it alive, or even if we do, it's going to be a coincidence. We hunt it down the old-fashioned way, and we kill it. Thing's gonna leave a trail. They want proof? They'll still have it. They just won't get to talk to it."

Hill shook his head. "Goddammit, that fucker killed Pappy," he added. "He was a good man, damn it. He did not deserve to die that way."

Pulver leaned back in his seat and nodded his head, not saying a word.

Tomlin looked at the man and asked, "You okay with that?"

"Hell yeah," Pulver replied. "I want that bastard dead." He reached into his sack and started counting his small arsenal of grenades. "I'm *great* with it."

Above them the rains continued and the winds howled and the lighting thrashed the skies. It was going to be a long night. Tomlin felt it in his bones.

Pappy was dead.

That hit him as hard as losing Burke, King, Orologas, and Strand. The commander had been a mentor and a friend. Catching that creature had been his mission— his life's work. His death added fuel to their reasons for wanting the goddamned alien dead.

It was going to happen.

20

The skies over DC were calm, and the wind blew gently across the nation's capital. It was a good night.

Woodhurst was sitting in his room with the window open enjoying the cool breeze. He looked around and smiled. This was going exactly the way he'd wanted. Three conversations since they'd received the images from Elliott, and suddenly they had the attention of all the right people. He could practically hear the wallets opening.

It wasn't about money—except that it was. Much as he hated that, he understood it, and now he was on the side of the coin he preferred. Most likely there would be limitations, but he doubted there would be any more cuts.

Having proof of an alien meant that suddenly he was no longer a pariah. Having an actual alien made all the difference in the world. There had been talks about the need to tighten the belts, to make sure that everyone did all they could to keep spending down.

Stargazer was well equipped, but the continuing cuts

had taken a toll on acquiring new equipment and getting the replacement parts they needed. It was difficult for a strike team to work without the right tools, and it was impossible for security to be a consideration when the men doing the examinations had to send out for tests on the captured creature.

It hadn't gotten so bad that they couldn't perform the fundamental procedures, but one of the shots Pappy sent clearly showed a wound bleeding a luminescent green, instead of a dark red. That required outside facilities, but how the hell was someone to get a sample examined properly if the techs at the remote lab were freaking out over the glow-in-the-dark goo in the vial?

And they had to consider the possibilities of contamination. Elliott had fought hard for the decontamination room, and he'd won that fight, but the cost had been prohibitive. That had all been theoretical, making it that much harder to justify the funds. Given that they now had an alien in their possession, Woodhurst had to seriously consider the possibility that even a sneeze from the damned thing could lead to a global pandemic.

Several of his people had faced off with the alien without any protection whatsoever, and it worried the hell out of him.

There were images of the nightmare with and without the war mask it sported. Woodhurst remembered the discussions he'd had with Elliott over the years and was stunned by how much the man had remembered. It had been half a lifetime and he'd recalled the size of the thing, the savagery of its form, and where it wore armor, and what sort of weapons it carried. There had been times when he'd doubted Pappy's recollections.

He owed the man an apology and a good meal.

Traeger had gone to bed already, preparing for the next day. He probably should have followed the younger man's example, but his mind was too active to even consider sleep. There was brandy in his room, but he tried to avoid falling into that trap. He had seen the mark it had left on Elliott. Poor bastard.

Despite that, the man had cause for celebration. Pappy had been vindicated. After years of attempts and failures, the old man would finally be able to look at the rest of the people in the Company and tell them to go suck eggs. He had succeeded despite the claims that what he'd seen had been a lie. He'd managed what no one before him had accomplished—he'd found living proof of the aliens who came here and waged their covert war on the human race.

They had a living specimen, and it was guaranteed to make the cash flow in order to keep Stargazer afloat. He suspected that within the next day or so he'd be talking to the president of the United States about plans for the future.

While he was considering the possibilities, his phone rang—not the cell phone in his pocket, but the one on his nightstand. There were only a handful of people who even knew where he was, which meant he was instantly alert.

"Woodhurst."

"Hello, General. This is Andrea Laurel." The voice was calm and collected. "I thought we should have a conversation."

Woodhurst forced the smile from his voice. Senator Andrea Laurel was one of the heavy hitters in DC. He'd known her for many years, and her party was in control, but she was the rarity in the current hierarchy in that she appeared to be immune to bribery. When she voted for anything, it was because her constituents wanted it. If the woman was taking any money on the side, the paper trail was hidden too well to find it.

"Senator," he said, "it's good to hear from you. How can I help you?"

"Well, General, I think it's the other way around," she answered. "I'm not calling so you can help me. I'm calling to give you a warning."

"A warning?" He didn't like the sound of that. Warnings were for when everything wasn't going in your favor, and so far the day had been extremely favorable.

"William Traeger."

"Traeger?" Woodhurst frowned. "What about him?"

"Will had a follow-up with me earlier today, General," she said. "When we talked yesterday, most of the discussion covered how much the entire Stargazer Project was in danger of buckling, without a little support. Excuse me, that's backwards isn't it. Project Stargazer."

"Not to worry, Senator. As long as the project still operates you can call it whatever you want." He hoped that sounded like a joke, but wasn't sure. Not many people made Woodhurst nervous, but Senator Laurel could make or ruin the project with just a few well-placed words.

Laurel chuckled softly. "Yes, well, the problem, General, is that young Traeger came to see me again today, and he brought along a few very convincing photos."

Ah, so that's it, he thought. "Yes, we just made the acquisition this morning."

"Which is wonderful, I'm sure, and it works to your benefit, believe me." She paused, likely for effect. "No, the point I want to make is that he's apparently got a few notions about the chain of command for your project."

"How do you mean, Senator?" His ears rang with a high, tinny noise. Traeger was trying to unseat him. He didn't need to hear the details to know it, but he'd listen just the same.

"William Traeger is a company man, and you already know that. He is also ambitious on levels that would make me worry if he was actually running for a seat in Congress. He'd make me very nervous, actually."

Woodhurst nodded, but said nothing. The senator was working her way toward a point and would get there at her own pace.

"General, putting it in direct terms, Traeger is trying not only to buy the backing for Stargazer, he's trying to remove you and a few other people from the equation. He danced around the amount, but he essentially offered me compensation in the form of promises to give subcontracts to companies in which I own a decent share, and promises to offer them the first crack at advanced technologies." She paused again for a moment. "Make no mistake here, General, he was offering incentives not only to keep Stargazer funded, but to move him into a position in charge of the operation The two were unquestionably tied together."

It wasn't quite a pain in his chest—more like a sudden lump that made swallowing more difficult. Woodhurst considered it a warning sign, just the same.

"I appreciate you letting me know, Senator."

"We go back a long ways, General. I don't see any reason for you to be punished because some young Turk wants to climb a few levels higher than he should."

"Just the same, you certainly didn't have to go through the trouble, and I appreciate it."

"Well, if you want to you can just put a check in the 'owed one' column and call it done." Then she added wryly, "Or you can just return the favor if ever it comes up."

"That I will, Senator." Woodhurst nodded and tried to ease back the pressure he felt on his hand as it tried to crush the life from the phone. "I look forward to seeing you at the meeting tomorrow."

"I'll see you then, General."

Woodhurst set the phone back in its cradle and sighed. The day had been going so well…

21

At least the downpour had stopped, and the sky had cleared. While the rain had helped to hide him, it also had hampered his progress in a critical way.

It wasn't as easy to hide himself without his cloaking device. Still, he had advantages over the local life forms. For one, his body had a certain level of natural camouflage. The patterns had benefitted the Yautja for thousands of years, when it came to hiding in a wide range of foliage. The coloration was paler than a lot of the local flora, but close enough that if he stood still in the greenery, he was harder to spot.

Not that he would take that chance. Rather than risking running along the paved trails leading back to his ship, he looked at the stars and let them guide him as he moved through the trees and the heavy, swampy areas. He startled more than a few birds, but few of the humans seemed to notice even when he was moving past them in close proximity.

There were a few exceptions, of course. Two individuals walking a four-legged creature on a long leash turned and listened when the animal started barking. Either they let the creature go deliberately or one of them was careless. In any event the animal charged toward him, barking and making threatening gestures. The size of the creature was close to half that of the dominant species, large enough to make it a valid threat, and when it came for him it bared very serious teeth.

The throwing disc punched through the beast's skull before he considered whether or not it was worthy of a kill. Hearing the beast's masters coming closer, he quickly pulled himself up into the branches of a tree.

The two owners called for "*King*" several times without getting a response. When one of them spotted the animal's cooling corpse, he had no choice but to silence them both. As they reached "King," he dropped down and landed on one of them, shattering the bones in the soft thing's back and neck. The disc in his hand sliced across the other's throat and silenced it before it could make a sound.

There would be no trophies. This was not hunting. This was survival. He had consumed the meat of the local creatures before, and though he found it unpleasant, there was a need to keep going and that meant sustenance. He skinned the thigh of one of the creatures and had a hasty meal before preparing to depart. He dragged all three corpses through the trees and dropped them into the waters of the closest marsh, and then he was on his way again.

When the stars faded away and the local sun rose, he

used its position to keep his path true. He moved at a rapid pace, though he was near exhaustion.

The sun rose higher into the sky as he slipped into the waters of a slow-moving river that was heavily populated with fish and the occasional reptilian hunter. He had already proven himself against one of the great lizards and now, instead, he remained wary of them.

The lack of his visor was maddening. The lack of his control gauntlet was worse. He could have called the ship to him. As he did so, he could have activated the plasma caster and eliminated all threats. Instead he was forced to rely on the old ways, which his father would have said were the best ways. It was draining, but it was also exhilarating.

N N N

The sun set and clouds covered the sky in a dark, threatening blanket. It would storm soon. He knew that much.

The elements always presented a level of danger. He could not hunt lightning, or slay a flooding river—it did not care about a plasma bolt, and when his ship was so far away, there was always a possibility that he could drown. That was part of the thrill of hunting in a new place. There were always challenges to consider.

The winds increased in intensity until they roared and shook the trees, and he moved on, sliding between the foliage as best he could while moving at a steady pace.

Finally he reached an area that was familiar. A copse of trees where he had carefully made a few directional marks, the sort that would be overlooked by anyone who didn't know what to look for. The scratches were small, but distinct.

N N N

Daylight had returned by the time he found his ship, but it could not be clearly seen past the heavy clouds and constant rain.

A voice command and the door of the vessel opened, dropping to allow him access. The vessel's cloak shimmered and stuttered through the process. Once inside he moved as quickly as he could, gathering what he needed. A new command gauntlet. A new bladed gauntlet. The old mask he had worn on a dozen previous hunts, damaged and scarred but still fully functional. Another Combistick and a plasma caster.

He could not allow the indigenous creatures to keep his property—he would have it back. He would hunt down and destroy the ones that sought to keep him as a prize and examine him. Such treatment was unforgiveable.

Conducting a quick scan he discovered something that quickened his pulse. He'd been compromised, and after a few moments he managed to find the device that someone had attached to his shoulder. It was almost undetectable, and he removed it with one quick stroke of a surgical blade.

It was a small thing, very likely with a limited range, but he thought he could still use it to his advantage.

There was time left, but not much. The hunt was almost finished. His trophies were few, but the hunt itself had been rewarding. He had even acquired data about the culture of these primitive animals. Until this expedition, he had never really considered that they had hunters, too. Now he knew.

That changed the challenge, in a profound way. It was

far more interesting to be the predator and the prey at the same time.

N N N

"What the fuck do you mean, 'the target is missing?'" Traeger's voice was soft, but only because he made himself speak calmly instead of roaring.

For the moment he could maintain his composure, because he had the photographic evidence he needed to make his point, and he'd shown it around without any hesitation. If Elliott hadn't come through, his wrath would have been epic.

He was back in his room after several last-minute meetings, and he'd been feeling pretty damned good when LaValle called him. He'd expected it to be Church, but apparently the man was handling problems on the home front instead of actually doing the hunting. He'd have a chat with him about that when he got back to the base.

"Look, it's not all bad news," LaValle said. "We have a team ready and we have an advantage."

"There's always a team ready, asshole. They're called the fucking Reapers."

"Yeah, okay. So the Reapers are out there, and they're looking, but they don't have all the best information, okay?"

"What do you mean?"

"I mean the damn thing has a tracker. It's one of ours. We have the code. We can activate."

Traeger took a deep breath and exhaled slowly. "All right. Okay. Now we're talking. The Reapers are already gone?"

"Yeah. They slipped out of isolation as soon as it happened."

"Doesn't surprise me. They're all worried about honor and pride. We don't have to worry about shit like that. We just have to worry about getting back our new acquisition."

"That's it," LaValle confirmed. "We've got the tools. We've got a team heading out."

"Good, excellent. Make sure they get to our Predator before the Reapers do."

"'Predator?'"

"Have you looked at that thing, LaValle? Does it look like a vegetarian to you?'

"Thing's got all the good looks of a crab, or a spider."

"Predator is good enough. Go get my Predator, LaValle, and don't disappoint me."

"Not gonna happen," LaValle replied. "We'll have it soon enough. Where can it go? We've got it tagged."

Time for a quick lesson. "You had him tagged and strapped before and he got away," Traeger replied. "What good did that do? Go get him, and don't fuck it up."

He killed the conversation.

The Predator was a must-have, but just as importantly, he needed to make this happen without the Reapers. It had to be on his terms. He needed to prove that the Company was as good as it needed to be in order to finish what he'd just started.

The skies outside were clear to the north, but when Traeger looked south he saw a line of darkness obscuring the horizon. Storm clouds blocked his view, save for an occasional dance of lightning within the very heart of that storm.

There was nothing more he could do except pray, and that was one lesson he'd never learned from his momma. Prayer was for the weak and the desperate, and he refused to be either.

Hours to go. He should have been nervous, but Traeger felt confident. He knew he'd done his best and his best was—with very rare exceptions—always enough.

22

The sun was up, the rain had set in again, and they were tired, but none of the Reapers thought about resting. There was a monster out there. They'd caught it before and they'd catch it again, though this time they wouldn't be worried about bringing the damned thing in alive.

Hill said nothing. He had his eyes closed and he was resting as much as one could without being asleep. Tomlin knew the man well enough to know that if he so much as whispered, Hill would be up and active.

He didn't test the theory.

They sped down Highway 41, staying close to the water whenever they could and heading for the last place where they'd seen the alien hunter. They'd seen evidence of its passing, subtle signs that most people would have missed. A branch broken here, a spot in soft mud. There was no time for closer examination. The marks were hard enough to distinguish in the rain, but Tomlin had no doubt that Hyde was right. He was a hunter and a killer, and he was the best tracker they had left.

No time for taking chances. The alien was out there and heading for whatever passed as a base camp. Maybe it planned to go home. Maybe it planned to call in reinforcements. It was hard to say. All they knew for certain was that no one had ever successfully captured one of these things in the past, and it would do whatever it could to end this contest without anyone having hard evidence that it existed.

Because if the situation were reversed, he would be doing the exact same thing.

That meant it would be hunting them down, taking out the Stargazer base if it had to. They needed to get to it before it could get to them.

"There." Pulver nodded and pointed with his chin. "We need to cut off the main road and head into the Okefenokee Swamp, I think."

"Is that the best approach?"

"It's not the fastest, but if we want to see signs of where it's headed, then 41 isn't going to do us much good. The road here veers away from the swamp, and most of the attacks took place pretty damned close to the waters. The thing won't be following the populated routes, either."

Tomlin nodded. The man wasn't wrong. He just didn't really like the idea of getting away from the main road. He wanted faster, and 41 was going to be faster than the dirt roads and warped pavement.

N N N

The side road—he couldn't even make out a sign that offered a name—was every bit as bad as he'd feared. Even with a reinforced suspension, they had no choice but to drive slower and to use caution. There were places where the heavy rainfall had washed the road away, or buried it under muddy waters that would only grow deeper.

Hill opened his eyes, looked at their surroundings and growled, just as annoyed as Tomlin.

Hyde was the most active of them, scanning every tree they passed and searching for any signs that a seven-foot-tall alien might be hiding nearby, or at least that it might have passed this way. There was nothing. Even if they were following the exact same path, the creature was canny.

Above them a nearly silent military copter tore the air apart, heading south. They knew the bird well enough, having traveled in one before. Someone other than the Reapers had left Stargazer with a mind toward finding and capturing the thing they'd already taken down once.

"Who do you think it is?" Hyde's voice was startling in the silence.

"Modified HAL LCH," Pulver answered, "Army or CIA—either way, they've got a nice lead on us."

Hill shook his head. "They don't have shit. They're just doing the same job as us, and they got birds while we got wheels."

Tomlin said, "Anything is possible. We don't know what they did to that thing while we were locked away. Maybe they've got trackers. Maybe they have a damned GPS satellite aimed at it right now."

"No way to know," Hill responded, "but I say we do our best to follow those guys if we can."

Tomlin nodded and gunned the engine a bit more than he was comfortable with. They didn't want to lose out on the hunt, but he also knew they failed immediately if he wrecked the transport.

The rains picked up again and the wipers moved furiously to allow him to see past the water smearing the windshield. Hill sat up, suddenly alert, and kept his eyes on the side of the road, while the other two did the same thing.

They moved as quickly as they could, the wind and the rain playing havoc around them.

N N N

LaValle peered toward the ground below, ignoring the furious winds that made his stomach churn and the nearly continuous wash of hard rain that obscured the view. On the screen in front of him a small dot blinked constantly, indicating that their target was no longer moving.

"I think we might have just gotten lucky, gentlemen." He looked at the pilot, a man he'd known for more than a decade, and then looked back at the soldiers in the black helicopter. There were markings on the vehicle, of course, but they were lies. According to those markings it belonged to a company that did emergency repairs in remote areas. The company was on the New York Stock Exchange, but never did enough movement to look even remotely sexy to the average investor.

It was a good cover, and it helped the Company move where it needed to without anyone getting too curious.

Not that he expected too many people would be popping their heads out of the windows in this weather. Besides, in comparison to the average helicopter used by the state and local authorities, this thing made only a whisper of noise.

"Got a location for me?" Rodriguez, the pilot, looked away from his controls only for a moment, and even then his hands held a death grip on the flight stick.

"Sending it right now." The tap of a button and the coordinates were sent to Rodriguez. The pilot nodded and made corrections.

"Fifteen minutes out. Looks like it's gonna be near Deer Water Springs."

"What the hell is Deer Water Springs?"

"Very small town. Like one paved road, a handful of buildings."

"Then maybe our luck is holding." LaValle allowed himself to smile. It was good to catch a break or two. He needed them. They needed them. He understood what Traeger was up to—he was one of the few. Most of the men with him were loyal to the Company and they'd all been loyal to Elliott. The old buzzard had been the butt of a few jokes in his time, but that had changed the moment the Predator had been brought in.

They'd been ready to volunteer for the job the instant Pappy's body was discovered. It was hard not to want to make amends for any harm they'd caused the poor bastard over the years, even if the harm had all been muttered comments and the occasional joke in poor taste.

So, yes, they were here to capture the Predator. They were also here to make sure they felt a little better about themselves when it was all said and done, and LaValle supposed that included him as well.

The winds were hellish and he held on tightly to the bar above his head as Rodriguez compensated for the latest hard gusts. LaValle's stomach tried to churn and he refused it that luxury. There was too much at stake for him to puke his guts out. He'd save that for after everything was done.

Despite the conditions that tried to wash them from the sky, Rodriguez managed to land in a clearing not far from their target. There were lights out there, garish lights that flashed in a dozen different colors and, unless he was mistaken, there might actually be a Ferris wheel just past the closest copse of trees.

"Are we near an amusement park?"

Rodriguez shook his head. "Looks like a county fair set up, and not even a big one. Odds are there's no one even there in this weather."

"Well, isn't that just shits and giggles." LaValle looked at the men with him and gestured for them to get themselves ready.

"Hey, it's light," Rodriguez said. "Beats total darkness."

"Not always, but probably in this case," LaValle admitted.

They cleared the copter a few minutes later and headed in the direction of the fairground where, according to the tracker, their target was waiting. There were no pep talks. They knew what they were there to do.

The Reapers had been handicapped by the need to bring their prey in alive. These men weren't the Reapers, and LaValle didn't feel that particular compulsion. Dead or alive was fine with him, and if they could locate the alien's ship, well, that was just going to be a big old cup of gravy to wash down their meal.

The air hissed as the hot rain shifted and blasted down hard enough to make him blink past the waters bouncing from the brim of his cap. They all were soaked in seconds, and not a damned thing to be done about it. The only advantage he could think of was that their intel said the aliens saw in the infrared spectrum. If that was true, the rains might well make it harder for the creature to spot them. A little camouflage in the form of warm waters hiding their heat trails.

The county fair rides glowed weirdly in the downpour—vague, brightly lit shapes. There was no clear paved access to the grounds, but there were mud trails where people had walked through the local greenery and trodden it down into the muck. LaValle had the men split into two separate groups and approach the lighted area from different directions. The Predator was supposed to be a keen hunter, and it seemed foolish to offer it a single target.

The shapes became more cohesive the closer they got. At first a few trash cans and empty stands that offered fry bread, games of chance, and hamburgers—or would have if the place was actually up and running. Badly painted signs on plywood surfaces, open-faced booths with canvas tops that were snapping and sputtering in the hard winds and rain. He could remember a dozen similar carnivals from when he was a kid, but none had seemed so menacing. Somewhere nearby a creature was very likely hunting for them.

Murphy, his second in command, ducked low and very nearly crawled as he reached the first stand and moved behind it, checking for any hint of an enemy. He came back out a few seconds later and started toward the next stall, gesturing for Hamilton to do the same on the other side of the clearing. Hamilton nodded and ran to a ring toss. The winds had knocked over most of the glass bottles in the center island. There was a completely irrational sense of satisfaction in that. LaValle had never been any good at ring tosses.

Hamilton moved with slow precision as he examined the entire stand and then moved for the next game of chance.

Murphy didn't emerge from his latest stall.

LaValle felt the hairs on his neck rise. No one spoke, but they all looked to him for direction. He gestured for a halt and then waved two others to join him at the shooting gallery, where several waterlogged air rifles waited for someone to use them against battered tin targets.

Nothing.

There was no one in the booth. That was a problem. Murphy should have been there, and he was not.

LaValle looked carefully around the area. One of the others—Brown, was it?—pointed at a spot near the back of the booth. A dark pool was quickly spreading into a larger puddle. LaValle felt his skin crawl into gooseflesh.

Was it possible? Moving closer he saw the water-soaked footprint that belonged to nothing from this planet. There were too many toes, and they were in the wrong places. Also, the print was enormous, several inches longer than his size ten.

Brown—Anderson? Carter?—he hated forgetting names. The guy gestured toward the dumpster set behind the row of stalls, silently asking if he should check it out. LaValle nodded a quick yes and looked up toward the trees above, as the rains kept crashing down into his face.

It was hard to see anything up there, but the branches on the closest weeping willow seemed to sway against the direction of the wind. It had to be his imagination. Looking at the thin branches, he couldn't imagine them holding his own weight, let alone the weight of a creature that stood seven feet tall.

Brown came toward him with a grim expression on his face. He pointed at the waste container.

"There's blood and a lot of it. No body."

LaValle shook his head and felt his lips press together.

Not ten feet from him, Brown's abdomen exploded in a spray of blood. Whatever the hell hit the man couldn't be seen—it was a vague blur in the downpour. LaValle didn't even have a chance to blink before the men with him were firing just past the dumpster.

The waste receptacle weighed in at a few hundred pounds, at least, but it moved toward them as something shoved it in their direction. The wheels under the thing squealed loudly in protest, and the entire shape wobbled. Every last one of them got the hell out of the way as it rumbled into the ring toss and caused the structure to collapse entirely.

Four men scattered in different directions, moving on instinct, and LaValle could do nothing to prevent them from breaking ranks. Hamilton ran to the left, but focused on the area just past where the dumpster had started its journey. He might have seen something, he might simply have decided not to take any chances. In any event, he fired in short, controlled bursts that didn't seem to hit anything.

After that, there was only the sound of the storm.

No one spoke, no one fired, but the rains hissed their way to the ground and the winds let out angry whispers as they moved through the trees and across the snapping canvas of the carnival.

"Fuck this," LaValle growled. "Spread out. Keep your eyes open. It's got camouflage technology. We don't. That means if you see someone in black clothes, you don't fucking shoot." The men nodded and did as they were told. Each looked around intently, keeping their weapons at the ready.

⩘ ⩘ ⩘

The rains would have the local creatures half hidden from his view, if he had been dependent only on his natural vision. He adjusted, moving into the ultraviolet spectrum, and saw his prey clearly enough.

It would be easy to dispatch them from a distance. Too easy, and so he moved carefully, knowing that the hard rains would splash off of his body and render him more visible than he usually was. That did not mean the creatures would spot him—only that they had a chance.

The blade disc appeared in his hand, a deadly array

of curves. He aimed carefully before letting loose. The weapon whirled and soared and buried itself deep in the side of one of the black-clad creatures. It did not have a chance to scream before it was dead.

A moment after that the others saw their companion fall, and immediately raised their weapons, trying to locate him. While they fluttered and moved, he stepped close to a second target and drove his blades deep into the creature's torso, cutting bone and meat alike as he lifted the screaming thing and then tossed it at its nearest companion.

The dying one thrashed and screamed, and the one on which it landed did the same, while firing its weapon without caution. The projectiles from the device hit only air and structures, but the noise and risk had the rest of the small gathering scattering in an instant, calling out to the one who fired carelessly.

They died so easily. It would be tempting to grow careless, but he would not allow it.

One of the creatures spotted him. It aimed for him and opened fire. He did his best to avoid being hit, and failed. The bullets pounded through his left shoulder and tore chunks of meat away. He screeched and dropped to the ground, rolling to get away from the fiery pain.

The best intentions failed in that moment. He would have preferred to hunt them down with Combistick and blades, but the mounted plasma caster on his shoulder was there for a reason, and he changed tactics as the blood flowed out of his arm. Three of the things were still moving—the one he'd knocked aside and two that had not yet been touched. The first of them, the one that had hit him successfully, took a plasma blast to the head and the body fell to the ground, flesh steaming where it touched the puddles of fallen water.

The next one took aim at where the bolt of energy had originated, but by then he had already moved on, sliding to the side and watching carefully to see if either of the remaining targets knew where he was. They did not, or if they did, they hid that fact by facing the wrong direction.

The telescoping spear cut through the air effortlessly and the Combistick did its work, slamming through the armor and breast of the one aiming close to where he was standing. It wailed out its pain and clutched at the shaft, pulling desperately. It fell, shuddering and making high whining noises.

The last of them fired wildly.

He ducked low as the blood flowed from his shoulder. He would need to mend that. First, however, there was one left to kill.

In its panic the creature ran directly toward him. Rather than attempt to kill it with a weapon, he reached out and caught the thing by its thick neck. It grunted and tried to raise the firearm. He caught the hand holding the weapon and bent it back until muscles and cartilage parted and bones broke.

There was a distinct satisfaction to killing with his hands. It fought and tried to break free, its arm pounding ineffectively against his forearm and elbow. Had the beast been of a better size it might have wounded him more, but it was small and panicked and it died as he broke its neck.

He gathered the bodies and hauled them to the side. He hoped to return and claim trophies, but not yet. There was too much to do. A quick look around and he gathered three of the weapons the creatures carried, removing their primitive missiles. Pulling a vial from a pocket, he used the chemical it contained to melt the metal and change its properties until, finally, he could cover his wounds. He stifled a scream at the blazing pain, daring not to attract the attention of his adversaries. They were primitive, but they were hunters, and while he had scattered them, this dominant species often ran in packs. They would regroup, and there might be more.

Packs could kill far too easily.

Slowly the pain faded down to a tolerable level and he breathed deeply, resting in the heavy warm rain as lightning started in the distance. It cut a path through clouds and rain alike, and moments later the thunder exploded.

More distractions. Good.

He was careful as he rose and gathered his weapons. The hunt was not over, and his best weapons had been taken. They were locked away, though not for much longer.

N N N

The rains were getting worse, not that LaValle cared. He looked at his pad and was grateful for the waterproof case. They moved quietly, carefully, only four of them left. The rest, judging from the sounds they'd heard, were likely dead.

That hadn't been the plan and it sure as hell wasn't acceptable. They had a task set to them, and they'd finish it. The only good news was that the bastard was nearby. They could locate it, but it didn't have the same advantage. If they could just stay alive, they might catch the Predator off guard and finish this.

He didn't like it when things went wrong. LaValle was a rational man, and he preferred a rational world. The idea of invisible aliens somehow *offended* him.

The men listened and moved as a tight group until they approached a concession stand with a heavy canvas body. The winds snapped and rippled the thing, but it still stood. And, according to his tracking device, their prey waited inside.

No words were spoken. LaValle moved toward the opening and beckoned the others to follow, crouching low to the ground as he slipped inside. His skin felt too tight and his heart thudded angrily in his chest, waiting for a spear or a claw or some other disturbing weapon to pierce his Kevlar armor and cut through his body.

Had he ever needed to pee so badly in his life? He had doubts.

The tarp above him drummed on with the sound of the rain and he moved as quickly as he could, alert for any sign of the alien. To his surprise there were a couple of bare bulbs offering some light. When he reached a corner he looked again at his tracker's signal. According to the red dot the damned thing was close enough that he should have been able to smell it—but there was *nothing*.

Around him the others moved through the small tent. It wasn't designed to hold many people, and half of the interior was taken by a refrigeration unit and a deep fryer that had long since cooled off. His men stationed themselves in the corners.

"There's no one else," one of them said, keeping his voice low. "If that thing was here it would have killed us all by now."

LaValle felt his lips press together. "Well, it *was* here, and the signal says it's almost on top of me. I mean, like within three feet, but—" He cursed softly under his breath and reached up to the support beam that held the place upright, despite the wind's best efforts.

"Fuck me." The tracker was resting in the post, half hidden because the bastard alien had taken the time to dig a hole in the wood and carefully stow it away. He pointed to the tracker and made sure his men saw it. They had been outsmarted by the thing out in the stormy weather.

This was likely to get even messier.

23

The committee members sat in their chairs in the elaborately decorated conference room where there were no cameras or visitors allowed. There were seven members in total, and they sat at a small dais that elevated them above the two men they now faced.

The members were silent as they listened to the reports given by first General Woodhurst and then by William Traeger.

Woodhurst carefully outlined what everyone already knew—that there were aliens who came to the planet from time to time and hunted humans, and that the evidence was rare but significant. He also reported that one of the creatures had been captured and managed to escape, leaving behind significant technological items that were currently being examined and researched, even as multiple teams of professionals went after the creature.

Traeger got to explain that the escaped alien was on foot, and that the pursuers had a tracking device implanted in the creature's flesh. Though they had not yet captured the Predator—his term, which the committee used when they started asking questions—the recapture was imminent.

Woodhurst showed the pictures of the alien, handing around close-ups of the face with and without helmet in place, and images of the various items taken from the thing, including an array of small skulls that were decidedly not Terran in origin.

The general was pleased, but he was guarded. And then the questions started. Senator Raferty spoke first, a thin smile on his broad face.

"General, how is it that a creature you've been actively hunting for well over five years managed to escape your confinement? Doesn't that strike you as strange, given the timing of these events?"

Woodhurst leaned forward in his seat and pinned the man with his gaze. There were many things that could be said about the general, but he never flinched from tough questions.

"That's something I'm looking into, Senator," he said with calm confidence. "The creature was sedated and yet, by the looks of things, it managed to cut through its restraints, perhaps with the claws you can see in the images. It should have been unconscious. The best calculations from four separate doctors, including a xenobiological specialist, suggested that the sedation used would have left the thing very nearly comatose."

He leaned back.

"I should point out," he continued, "that the creature

in question killed members of a well-trained and heavily armed security force. This is just an example of why we need to continue funding for Project Stargazer. If one of these things can cause as much damage as this alien did, we need to be prepared, should they ever be encountered again."

The senator nodded, a small frown marring his round features as he thought—or acted as if he were thinking—very seriously on the general's words. After a moment he spoke again.

"And given that this… this Predator… escaped on your watch, what makes you think you are the right person to be in charge here?"

"He didn't escape on my watch," Woodhurst replied. "Frankly, I was here, trying to once again garner the necessary funds to continue the Stargazer program, as well you know." He stared hard at the man. "He escaped under the careful watch of Roger Elliott, one of the driving forces behind Project Stargazer. Commander Elliott gave his life in the effort to recapture the alien before it could leave the base."

"A sacrifice we are all keenly aware of, General," Senator Raferty replied. "Nonetheless, the Predator is now on the loose."

"Yes it is, and we are currently doing all that can be done to recapture a creature with far superior technological capability. A creature that is capable of interstellar travel, capable of cloaking its vessel to the point that our very best technology has not yet found a way to track it, and capable of using energy weapons that—as you have seen in previous reports—are capable of devastating an area over a mile in diameter.

"We currently have several of the creature's devices in our possession, Senator," he continued. "Not a perfect score, but for the first time we have the ability to examine some of that extremely advanced technology, and hopefully break it down and merge it with our own."

"Which will cost the United States taxpayers approximately how much, General?"

"That's not something we can yet estimate," Woodhurst said, "and it's not my department." He smiled as he spoke and then continued, "The benefits could be immeasurable. Whatever the cost, the rewards will justify it."

"What sort of rewards?"

"Soldiers who can move in and out of an area without ever being detected—those are soldiers who come home alive, Senator. They are also soldiers who win conflicts with very minimal losses to either side."

Raferty nodded, and the senator's lower lip pooched out as he considered the words.

Elizabeth Siegler, the representative who had fought hardest to keep the program afloat in the past, seized the opportunity to speak up.

"How soon before you can tell us that the Predator has been captured again or killed?"

"We're hoping to secure the asset quickly, of course, but I expect we'll know for certain within the next twenty-four hours." Woodhurst frowned. "Likely much sooner, as the teams sent for retrieval have tracking devices in place, and were in pursuit within minutes of its escape."

When Raferty spoke again his tone was different, accusatory.

"General, can you explain why you have a need for so much more financing than you've requested in the past?"

Woodhurst carefully avoided showing contempt for so idiotic a question.

"As has been stated, we now have definitive proof of an extraterrestrial threat," he said. "We need to train more soldiers to be able to handle that covert challenge, and we need facilities that have been upgraded to allow for better containment and decontamination. Frankly, while we have a facility that currently is capable of handling some of the risks that an alien life form presents, there are other aspects where we can't be sure we'll be so lucky."

"What do you mean?"

"I mean, Senator, that what might seem like a common cold to them could well be worse than the Spanish influenza epidemic that took place in 1918. We haven't yet encountered this problem, but that doesn't eliminate the possibility. There might be a pathogen that's so alien to us that it could wipe out huge swaths of the population." He paused to let that sink in.

"We need to increase our ability to study any possible biological threats, no matter how insignificant they might seem." He shrugged. "That's just the tip of it. Given the extraterrestrial's cloaking technologies, we may need additional satellites sent up that can properly track any incursion, should the creatures come back here again. Call it an ounce of prevention."

Senator Laurel looked grim, and spoke up.

"Are you saying that biological weapons are a possibility?"

"Not yet, not as far as we can tell, but we need to be prepared should these aliens—inadvertently or deliberately—bring a biological disaster down on us. You can see the mask that this thing was wearing; it was attached to a system that likely scrubbed the air. It might even be attached to a separate air supply, though it's not yet possible for us to tell yet. We still need to dismantle and study the devices in question."

They all looked uncomfortable. He was all right with that. They should be. For years they had engaged in theoretical discussions, building scenarios and even preparing for some of them. But until they'd actually *captured* one of the things, everything had been abstract. The realities were far more sobering.

The Spanish influenza epidemic had been so bad because the virus mutated and came back to the United States. The nation was completely unprepared for the changes, and in a single year the flu killed fifty million people worldwide. The thought that these aliens might bring something that could jump species was terrifying in the extreme.

Still…

"We're getting off track here," he said, pressing on. "The fact is, we have aliens coming to this planet. Not just rumors of aliens but actual creatures that have spent their time in the past hunting down and killing human beings. Near as we can tell they've done it for sport—no other explanation fits the facts. We need to be able to find and prevent these creatures from ever doing that again.

We also need to capture as much of their technology as possible to guarantee that we can defend ourselves. We need, simply put, to know what we are facing and how to deter it."

Woodhurst stood and looked at the committee members one at a time, and spoke very carefully.

"We must also consider that there's a real chance that their entire reason for exploring our planet, for hunting people down over the years, is to discover if we are ripe for a full-scale attack."

That made a few of them sit up.

"I'm not saying it's the only possibility, but it's one we have to consider. For all we know they've been monitoring us for centuries, and waiting for us to evolve enough to become a threat." He'd actually read that in a science-fiction story when he was younger, and it had stuck with him through his years. Was it probable? No. Possible? Of course. "We need to understand their technology as quickly and as completely as we can, and we need to prepare for any possible contingency." He sat back down.

There was silence for almost a full minute.

Traeger spoke up, softly, but his voice was clear enough.

"I've put together a proposal that each of you has had a chance to review. That proposal allows for a serious increase in the budgetary considerations for Project Stargazer and keeps the program entirely autonomous. No need to compromise security, no need to have still more discussions every time the standing POTUS decides it's time to allot monies to new pet projects." Traeger's smile was pure silk, and his voice was honey. The man didn't have to move a muscle to grab the attention of every person in the room—including Woodhurst, who felt his blood pressure rise like a high tide as the words were uttered.

The general wanted to call him out on this new proposal, but knew that if he did he'd seem weak in front of the committee. Laurel had warned him so that he could prepare and counter if he wanted, and so he could do so without looking like an ass.

"Privatization of any part of this program is risky, Will." He spoke softly. "Corporations have to answer to stockholders, and stockholders like to know where the money is being spent. A very close eye would have to be kept on what was said—to anyone at every possible level."

Traeger smiled. "Naturally, General. The good news is that the CIA is very good at keeping and maintaining secrets. The better news is that a guaranteed budget is easy when you can promise a return on investment. Not every item that the Predator brought us is something that can't be shared. Weapons, to be sure, and stealth devices, but there may be new energy sources, for example. Under the right circumstances, those sources could be used to improve the quality of life, and American companies could maintain a tight grip on their manufacture."

Traeger smiled and continued. "Hell, we could find medical uses for most of the technology in the helmet alone. New ways to scan diseased tissues, perform diagnostics. According to the reports we've already read, the creature's mask enables it to see across a much broader spectrum than human tech allows. There's no telling how far the applications may go."

Traeger leaned forward and stared.

Woodhurst leaned back, unblinking.

There it was, the look he'd half expected since the moment he met the young CIA agent. There was a deep and abiding hunger in those eyes. He'd hoped that, somehow, the man's lack of communication had been an oversight, but he was pretty sure he knew better.

"Let's not kid ourselves about the military ramifications, General," Traeger said, pressing his advantage. "We all know that stealth technology, weapons that cast energy bursts strong enough to melt steel, are just the tip of the iceberg. We could acquire an edge greater than we've had since the days when the US owned all the nukes, and everyone else was forced to behave.

"Under my plan, we can guarantee that every last one of those military contracts stays strictly within the United States and is watched over by the CIA. Nothing gets out. Nothing leaks. We all win."

"We can do that now, Will," Woodhurst said.

"But not with the proper autonomy." Traeger shrugged. "Presidents change. Congress changes, though not as often. If the current administration decides that everything should be manufactured in China, it all goes. That's the way it works. But if the private sector—carefully selected members, of course—are paying the bills, you can bet they'll fight to keep what's theirs right here on US soil. We don't have to ask permission, and no one has to lose sleep over the budget.

"How many times have you had to do this song and dance, General? Six? Ten? I'm just offering a solution that stops this from continuing to be a problem."

That damned smile again. So calm and collected.

"Private businesses do not change," Traeger asserted. "They might get new names, new personnel, but they all play the same game. Everyone answers to someone, General, and in this case they'd answer to us. We would be the final authority, decide what happens." Traeger tapped the edge of his still-full water glass. "The private sector will be grateful for the scraps we give them, and they'll pay handsomely to get in line for those scraps."

And there it was, the man's pitch to yank the power away from Woodhurst. Traeger didn't have to point out that the right person—in the right place, at the right time—could turn a handsome profit by investing in certain companies. Were there rules about insider trading? Yes, but every person in the room knew the loopholes.

Nor did Traeger need to say who the "right person" was.

General Woodhurst sat back a little further and contemplated his options. Pappy Elliott was dead, and he'd miss the man very much, but at that moment he cursed the bastard for bringing this Judas into the fold.

ℵ ℵ ℵ

Traeger walked from the room as calmly as he could. General Woodhurst was an old man, and not as much of a fighter as he wanted to believe he was. But he was also a man with very serious military clout.

Not surprisingly the general was waiting for him. His expression gave away nothing.

"Well done, Will."

"It's nothing personal, General. You have your job and I have mine. You're still a part of the team, if you want to be. I mean that." He looked the man over, and expected some response, but Woodhurst remained unreadable. "Listen, this is your baby. I know that and I respect that, but my superiors want to make sure that this is handled the way that they want it handled, and there isn't much I could possibly say or do to dissuade them."

"It would have cost you. I get that."

"So, as far as I'm concerned, this is still your baby. I'm just the buffer you have to deal with between funding and reality."

"'Between funding and reality?'"

"Yeah. You want something, it has to go through me, but we're on the same side here, General. We want the same things, though we might not agree entirely on the best way to get them."

Woodhurst nodded slowly, his eyes never moving away from Traeger's.

"I suppose I better pack my things."

Traeger nodded and smiled. The man was not happy, but he'd recover. He'd been offered a bone instead of a steak, but the general was hungry enough to take it.

24

The rains grew worse. Devon Hill looked around and shook his head as the SUV slowed to a stop.

"Do we have any idea where we're going?" Hill knew the answer, but he felt like asking anyway.

"We're there," Tomlin said, and he opened the driver's side door. "Grab your gear and let's get hunting."

The helicopter was equipped with all kinds of fail-safes to guarantee that civilians didn't pay it much attention, but that hardly mattered to the four of them. They'd followed it as best they could. They'd lost track of it a couple of times, but quickly picked up the trail again. On the best day their vehicle wasn't as fast as the copter, but they had made good time just the same.

Hill didn't much like it anyway. No promises of what they were going to run into. No guarantees that they'd driven out here for anything at all, really. There was a damned fine chance that they'd get to where they wanted to be just in time to see the Company men cleaning up after their prize.

It didn't matter, not really, but it did, damn it.

The Reapers wanted this, they wanted a win. *Needed* a win. They'd lost half the team to the damned thing and it had got away. Before it escaped, it killed Pappy, and that was unforgivable. He wasn't just a mentor. Not at the end of the day. He was the man who'd made them a team and trained them as best they could be trained—to fight something that wasn't human, that was a killing machine.

Hill took a deep breath and let it out slowly as he climbed from the vehicle and grabbed his supplies.

Being scared sucked, but being scared also meant he was alive and that he'd be alert and ready. He'd been scared on every single mission he'd ever taken. That wasn't going to change. He did what he needed to do on every single mission, and that wasn't changing any time soon.

The remaining Reapers pulled their weapons, checked them, and tucked them where they needed to go. There were lights in the distance, weird, bright, and garish, flickering in the rain and the hard winds. It wasn't a hurricane out here, but it felt like one. He staggered as a gust came through the trees and bent them down like a giant foot was pressing them toward the ground.

Pulver shook his head and muttered something under his breath. There were times when that would have had Hill calling him on it, but in this weather he could damn near yodel and no one would hear. Besides, this wasn't exactly a formal mission. They were supposed to be in lockdown.

So much for regulations, he thought darkly.

Hill wondered what would be waiting when they got back.

Tomlin waved a hand and motioned them forward. It was time to hunt the fucker down.

Water crept past armor, helmet, and uniform alike, soaking them as they headed for the neon lights and what looked like a Ferris wheel. Hill shook his head. Long as there weren't any clowns. He hated those fuckers.

ⁿ ⁿ ⁿ

LaValle shook his head and listened as the winds and rain threatened to knock down their meager shelter. The heavy canvas rippled and snapped and the entire tent swayed almost hypnotically, even as water managed to find a way through and drip across the interior. The lights flickered now and again, but so far hadn't completely failed.

"We gonna wait for the thing to come to us?" Ezquerra damn near had to yell to be heard over the building storm.

LaValle considered that question seriously. On the one hand, it *would* be easier if the thing came to them, and they could just work together to take it out. On the other hand, there was a very real chance that the thing was out there and watching them right now, waiting for them to make a move. Hell, it could have a space bazooka aimed at the tent, and that thought got his blood pumping and made his skin feel even tighter.

"No, we're gonna move out," he said. "Spread out and do your best to maintain radio communications. It knows we're here. We aren't going to be able to sneak up. Let's make sure it can't do that to us, either."

That was enough of a motivator. One by one they left the tent, each peering through the gloom and checking on whether or not there was a Predator waiting. If there was, they couldn't see it in the harsh rain.

Tanaka left first, moving out in a low crouch and heading for the far side of the small park, his head weaving left and then right as he scanned his surroundings. A moment later Anderson was on the move, heading in the opposite direction. The man only cleared about fifteen feet before he became an indistinct blur in the rain.

LaValle shook his head. How the hell were they ever going to spot the damned thing, now that it had removed the tracker? They couldn't even see each other from a dozen yards away. Then again, what choice did they have?

He spoke into the radio. "Be careful. Don't shoot each other, all right? I don't want that kind of paperwork to file."

Ezquerra nodded once and faded into the rain.

A moment later it was LaValle leaving, and he nearly flinched as the downpour soaked him again. The water was warmer than before, and the lightning, which had been present for a while, was closer—close enough that when he saw a strobe of light that erased the darkness, the thunder was less than a heartbeat behind and loud enough to rattle his eyes in their sockets.

Under normal circumstances it would have been time to abort the mission, but not this time. They had to get the alien back, and goddamned fast.

"I think I've got something." Despite the rain and wind Tanaka's voice was clear in his ear. "Definitely got something. It's trying not to move, but I can see it in the rain. Maybe twenty feet away. If you can converge on me, do it."

That was enough. LaValle seconded the command and headed in the same direction Tanaka had gone. He considered pulling down the heavy goggles on his helmet and switching to night vision, but the ambient light from numerous rides and displays would have damned near blinded him if he'd tried. It wasn't dark enough to make the transition.

A small arena had been set aside for bumper cars, which were currently lying inert and covered with canvas. His skin crawled at the thought of how easy it would be for the creature to hide among the unmoving vehicles.

The water falling from the brim of his helmet was an irritant, but not enough to obscure his vision. It if had been, he might not have had to watch Tanaka as he was murdered.

The man stood stock still in front of him, his weapon down at his side, and then he rose into the air in one swift, fluid motion. Even as LaValle watched, twin blades punched through Kevlar armor and glistened in the neon lights. Dark stains ran down the length of those blades and tainted the water that dripped from the soldier's twitching body.

Kenneth Tanaka. Wife Laureen, sons Ken Junior and Michael, first daughter on the way, and here he was, gutted like a goddamned fish by something that was hiding in plain sight. LaValle did not hesitate.

Taking aim at the air just above Tanaka's head, he fired three rounds and was rewarded by a shower of sparks and a loud pinging noise. Tanaka fell to the ground and splashed into a mud puddle, his body twitching, his face a mask of pain.

He was alive, the poor bastard.

From behind where Tanaka had been, the air warped and shimmered as lines of electrical discharge surged over the shape of the Predator. It couldn't be seen clearly, but it could be seen. Its war mask came into view, and LaValle thought he saw the fresh dent he'd managed to place over the left eye, and a matching dent across the forehead.

Pieces of a shape formed and vanished, leaving a picture painted from parts. Those parts made for a very large target. Knowing how big it was on an intellectual level wasn't the same as seeing the thing up and moving. That mask turned to stare at him as the wave of energy slowly hid it away again, and LaValle took the chance to fire again, aiming at the body beneath the dented visage.

Green blood exploded from the thing's fading arm and it roared, a deep warbling croak of a battle cry. Then it was moving. Adrenaline kicked into LaValle and a savage, primal thrill made him guiltily understand the excitement of the Predator's hunt. He'd wounded the bastard and it felt *good*.

As the Predator moved to one side, it faded from view.

LaValle did his best to stay calm as he looked at what was presented to him. The creature was missing, but it wasn't a ghost. It was just camouflaged better than any living nightmare had a right to be. He saw the water explode upward in a quick splash as one massive foot slapped down in the mud. Closer.

It was so damned much closer.

He set the rate of fire to fully automatic and aimed above that splash point. Bullets chattered and cut the air, but if the beast was hit, he couldn't see another splash of the nearly neon blood.

Then the thing hit him like a Mack truck.

One second he was firing, and the next his weapon was slapped aside as something unseen crashed into him from the left and launched him from the ground and into the air. He didn't land in mud, but instead crashed into the side of a bumper car, landing hard enough to rock the thing and very nearly knock it over. The force left him stunned. There was a loud crackling noise followed by a high-pitched whine—it was all the reception he got from his radio.

By the time he started to recover, the Predator was on him. He tried to move, but his body refused to listen to his demands. He could see the mud splashing closer, closer.

LaValle had always known the line of work he was in was dangerous, and he knew that, eventually, he would run into a situation where he wasn't on top. He'd just hoped there would be a few decades before it came to pass.

Then Anderson lifted a shotgun as he stepped over LaValle's body. He held the weapon in a proper position and pulled the trigger, unleashing an explosion of thunder. The flare from the barrel of the 12-gauge revealed nothing, but a secondary roar came back and a moment later the Predator was revealed.

Light arced and wavered around the creature's body. Near as LaValle could see from his prone angle, the alien hadn't actually been hurt by the shot, except perhaps for a few small wounds along the abdomen. The armor covering part of its broad chest had absorbed the worst of the damage.

Anderson pumped another shell into position and aimed. Before he could pull the trigger, the Predator reached out and grabbed the shotgun, close to the trigger, and twisted it sideways. Anderson let out a yelp as the alien's grip overpowered his.

The monster's other hand came down and drove a powerful fist into Anderson's helmet. The helmet lowered by a few inches, as did Anderson's head within it. Even over the rain and wind LaValle heard the man's neck breaking. He dropped, his arms twitching as he slumped into the muck. If he wasn't dead, he probably wished for death's release.

The shimmering image of the Predator began to fade again. Whatever had happened to make its cloaking abilities falter, it was apparently already fixing itself.

LaValle willed his arm to move, and this time it listened. He didn't try to stand up. Instead he gripped his Tavor TAR-21 and pointed the business end up at the spot where the creature was standing.

He pulled the trigger.

Nothing happened.

Either it was jammed or he'd run out of ammunition. Then the creature was gone, lost in that damn cloaking technology, so he didn't see what impaled his wrist and pinned his arm deep in the mud. He only knew it hurt more than anything he had ever felt before. LaValle felt his bile rise, and turned his head as his stomach rebelled. Nothing for it. The response was completely beyond his control.

He was dead and he knew it.

Ezquerra called out as he came closer. LaValle wanted to warn the man, but he was incapacitated. His stomach was still trying to void anything he might have consumed in the last few years, and his arm was pinned in place, locked against the mud. Prone as he was, LaValle was lucky to avoid drowning in his own puke.

The pressure didn't leave his arm, but as the Predator moved, the cloaking field apparently left the spear that pinned him in place. The metal point and shaft suddenly appeared. He did his best not to black out. He felt the world receding.

"Ezquerra!" he called out. "He's coming for you."

Ezquerra looked his way for just an instant. The man spoke, but whatever he said was lost in the wind, and the damned radio offered only a static hiss.

LaValle forced his arm upward, trying to dislodge the spear that had him stuck like a bug to the muddy ground. The pain was a mule kick to his senses and he felt the world wobble toward the gray again.

Shaking it off as best he could, he pulled. The spear rose up with a sick squelching noise and dropped roughly down. The force with which the spear hit the ground spread the bones in his arm and LaValle groaned deep in his chest, even as he watched his last remaining ally face off against the thing they'd come to kill.

The Predator showed itself to Ezquerra, then vanished again.

The man looked around, tried to find the creature, and it appeared with another quick rustle of blue energies. Hector Ezquerra was a big man, close to six feet two inches in height and nearly two hundred and twenty pounds of hard muscle. He was trained, a capable fighter who could hold his own against some very unpleasant odds—and had, more than once in the field.

Ezquerra was big, he was bad and he was dangerous.

He looked like an adolescent next to the creature.

He also wasn't a good man to startle. As soon as the creature showed itself, Ezquerra instantly drove a booted heel into the nightmare's knee. The armor over the thing's kneecap took the worst of the damage, but the blow was enough to make it lose its balance.

He lifted his pistol and fired point blank at the Predator's head. Instead the bullet found that damnable war mask again, though the impact sent the alien reeling back. Armor or no armor, the .45 caliber bullet carried a heavy impact. The thing let out another noise and staggered, catching itself before it could fall. Another deep wound scarred the metal surface of the mask.

Ezquerra took advantage of the moment and fired twice more, both bullets striking the mask again, and one of them, by design or happy accident, shattered the lens over the creature's right eye.

Then the Predator hit him in the chest and sent him sliding through the mud. When it struck, the soldier's armor did its job. Ezquerra stayed on his feet and remained functional despite being knocked several feet back. He got off another shot, which went wild. The one after that caught the Predator in the left shoulder, just under the small armor plate that covered the top of its arm.

LaValle pushed the spear through his arm, gritting his teeth and letting out a long whimpering screech as he freed himself. It hurt, oh, God, it hurt. The weapon slipped into the mud and was nearly buried under the torrent of water running for lower ground. He climbed to his feet, blinking back the rain. With his good hand he reached for the service pistol on his hip. It came free in his grasp and he sighted and aimed, ignoring the way his arm wanted to shake.

Ezquerra blocked a hard blow from the alien, but only barely. Where most men would have had their arm knocked aside by the savage strike, the Predator hardly moved. Instead of trying to fire again, Ezquerra stepped in closer and drove his elbow into the alien's abdomen.

That was a mistake. The attack would have probably worked on most people, but the Predator simply took the blow and then reached out with both hands, grabbing at the agent's head. Huge hands wrapped around Ezquerra's helmet and held it tightly.

Ezquerra pointed his pistol at the Predator's chest and fired.

The bullet tore into meat.

The Predator drove its knee up even as it hauled Ezquerra's head down. The helmet cracked in the nightmare's hands. What was left of Ezquerra's head leaked brains as the body fell to the ground. Fresh blood fell from the wound on the creature's chest, but it hardly seemed to notice.

Instead it looked toward LaValle and tilted its head, the one good eye on the mask a counterpoint to the dark wound where the other lens had been.

LaValle tried to aim his pistol.

The cannon on the creature's shoulder sent a flaming ball of energy for LaValle's face. It was the last thing he saw.

25

The National Weather Advisory called the weather over northern Florida and southern Georgia a tropical storm. The winds were harsh but not consistently bad enough to qualify as a hurricane. The rains were torrential, dropping more than an inch an hour. Lightning strikes were recorded at near record levels, and the warnings came out for people to stay in their homes if possible to avoid flash floods and wind shear capable of substantial damage.

It was bad enough that half of Coyahunga County was without power after the winds toppled four trees that took out power lines and one substation. It would be days before the power was fully restored.

In the area around Deer Water Springs, the water levels rose to dangerous heights, forcing the Army Corp of Engineers to release large quantities from the local reservoir to avoid a possible collapse of the outdated dam. The overflow washed out several smaller roads and kept the local police busy in efforts to redirect traffic and to aid the local power companies in attempting to repair downed wires.

All of which meant no one even cared what was happening at the local fair, which had wisely shut down when the storm warnings started. The Reapers carefully assessed the situation and prepared to enter what could only fairly be called a war zone.

✗ ✗ ✗

The hunt had been violent, but fruitful, and he gathered the trophies.

When it was done, he started back toward the ship and prepared for the tasks ahead. He was bloodied and he needed to attend to that before he could address the possessions that had been taken from him. The thrill of the hunt enabled him to barely feel the wounds, but they were still there and he was still bleeding.

Then he stopped.

There were more hunters in the area. Crouching behind one of the dilapidated structures, he saw them approach. Like the ones he'd eliminated, they were dressed in black garb, and heavily armed. They didn't see him—not yet— but they were looking, and they had to know he was close.

One last hunt then. One more fight before he collected everything he needed to collect. If he was too badly wounded by the time it was done, he'd set the self-destruct on both of his control gauntlets and let the explosions erase any evidence.

Quick patches were all he could manage for his new wounds. They would have to suffice. His Combistick was lost somewhere in the mud, but he retained other weapons, and he had his hands.

There were only four this time, but they wore devices over their faces that were likely to help them see in the semi-darkness of the storm. Taking one last look around, he moved to higher ground. Though he was being hunted, he would show them who was the prey.

This would all end soon enough.

He intended to be the only victor.

N N N

"So if I was a seven-foot-tall asshole from another planet that wanted to hunt humans, where the hell would I hide?" Hill's words were loud and clear over their radio link.

"No clue," Tomlin replied, "but we need to find this thing fast and we need to stick together. It's bound to be close." At least he hoped it was.

"That's an affirmative." Pulver pointed to a spot where a long metallic spear lay flat in the mud. There were no other indications that anything had happened there. Any evidence must have been washed away by the rain.

"We need to even the odds here," Tomlin said. "Pulver, can you find the generator and knock out the power? I don't know if the thing can see in the dark, but it can't hurt, and it might help."

"Understood. Let me see what I can find." The man started looking around, and then nodded. "About thirty yards ahead, right-hand side."

"Let's move in that direction."

They continued as a unit, each of them working to

cover his own designated area as thoroughly as possible. The alien *had* to be there. If it had already left, they were wasting time. This was their chance to get the bastard.

Hill tapped Tomlin's shoulder and pointed to a large ramshackle hut with a gaudily painted front end that said "Hall of Mirrors."

Christ, Tomlin thought, that was the last thing they needed—to try and find an invisible target in a room that barraged them with dozens of distorted reflections. He shook his head and motioned for them to continue.

Lightning cracked open the heavens and blinded them all for a moment, even as a deep bass roar of thunder shattered the hissing of the rain and the whooshing of the wind. The storm was getting worse, and they'd be lucky not to get fried.

"Seriously, where the hell *does* a thing like that hide?" Hill repeated, shaking his head as he looked carefully at every obstacle, every landmark. The ground was wet and sloppy, offering poor footing and hiding deep puddles.

"Anywhere it wants to," Tomlin answered. "It's got camouflage technology, remember?"

A few more yards and they reached the control box for the fairground, such as it was. As they approached they remained silent, and moved carefully. There were too many shadowy structures and draped tents, places where their quarry could be hiding. Places where things could go wrong.

There was a lock in place, but it wasn't secured. Pulver opened the box with ease. A minute later the entire carnival went dark.

"There," he said. "Maybe that will even the odds a bit."

Hyde shook his head and peered around again, using his night-vision goggles and trying to spot their target. Abruptly he snapped his fingers and pointed up toward the sky. Tomlin followed the gesture. All he saw was the dark shape of the Ferris wheel.

"What?"

"It's up there, on the—"

Then he dove out of the way as something hurtled toward them from above. A metal disc slapped into the muck. While it was still quivering Hyde was already up and moving, hauling ass for a different spot.

"Fuck!" Hill said. "It's above us!"

As if on cue the air crackled with artificial lightning. A ball of blue energy ripped through the air and narrowly missed taking him out. Hill ran forward and to his left. The ground where he had been standing exploded in a brilliant blue flash.

Pulver looked up at the amusement ride, pulled his arm back, and hurled something small and cylindrical.

"Don't look at it!"

Tomlin knew what was coming.

"Heads!" he shouted.

The grenade was small. It didn't have to be any larger. An instant later another blast of false lightning shattered the night, followed by a thunderclap. The flash-bang grenade lived up to its design as the sound shook the air and vibrated the bones in his chest.

Though no shape was visible, they all saw the resulting splash as the alien hit the ground. The wave of muck was impressive. It might have made their progress hazardous, but it also worked as a boon in this case, allowing them to know exactly where their quarry had landed.

Pulver tossed another flash-bang.

"Heads!"

This explosion was closer, close enough that even with his eyes closed, Tomlin saw a blue afterimage. The noise was louder, too, the *bang* painful even with his ears covered. There hadn't been time to put in earplugs.

When he looked up, all he could see was the spot where the mud was shaped roughly like a man. It looked like maybe Pulver's tactic had done some good. The thing wasn't yet moving.

Without waiting, Tomlin aimed and squeezed off a couple of rounds. One hit mud and sprayed upward. The second hit something that wasn't there and resulted in a quick spray of green luminescence.

An instant later the humanoid shape filled with water. The creature was gone. Lightning flashed through the sky, natural this time, and distracted him from trying to watch where the mud had shifted.

Pulver prepared to throw another flash-bang when the hand holding the grenade fell off at the wrist. Even with goggles on Tomlin barely saw the disc that took off the limb. It was like the one that had cut Orologas nearly in half.

The grenade hit the ground.

It was too close!

The light was enough to blind him through his eyelids. The explosion knocked him senseless.

*⁄ *⁄ *⁄

The world was a blur. His eyes refused to focus and try though he might, he couldn't hear anything beyond a thunderous ringing noise.

He tried to stand but his legs refused to move. He'd have been happy with crawling on his hands and knees, but that wasn't happening either. He wished he could remember his name or why he was lying face up in the rain.

Then it came rushing back.

Alien. Hunter. Killing.

Explosion.

With awareness came a pain that he'd managed to ignore. His hand was gone. He'd swung his arm to pitch the grenade, same as before, only this time when he watched to see if his aim was true all he saw was a jet of black liquid spurting from his wrist. Before he could figure out what the hell had happened, the world went fiery white and he was knocked to the ground.

"Ahhhhh. *Guh!*" It was all he could say. The pain crushed him under a ton of raw, screaming nerve endings. He still couldn't see worth a damn and his brain was drowning in sensory overload.

Warmth bled out of his wrist and across his chest. He looked down at the bleeding stump and reached with his remaining hand, growing aware of the fact that if he didn't staunch the blood flow he was as good as dead.

How the hell had this happened?

It had been going well. He was sure they had the damned thing on the ropes. Hell, it had fallen right in front of them, into the mud. That should have been it.

The world started to focus again and he looked up at the sky as the rain suddenly stopped dropping on his face. The goggles over his eyes were blurred by water, and so he used his good hand to wipe it away. He needed to see. Needed to know where the damned thing was and if it planned on killing him.

Everything above him should have been clear, but it was still distorted. The rain pounded down around him, but not where he was lying. It stopped before it could hit him in the face.

That distortion rippled and wavered and something that resembled a hand came down and covered his face. He couldn't really see it, but he could *feel* it as it covered his mouth and nose and eyes and pushed. His head slapped down into the mud and his helmet shifted.

Suddenly Pulver couldn't breathe. He could smell a cold, reptilian scent but he couldn't catch a decent breath. The pressure increased and he reached up with his remaining hand to push against the emptiness. It wouldn't move.

He tried to gasp, but couldn't. No air came to his lungs. Tried to scream but as soon as he opened his mouth the pressure shifted and he tasted a musky flavor and mud. Something cut into his scalp—claws—and shoved his helmet up and away from his face.

Pulver lashed out again with his remaining fist and hit the air, but it didn't flinch, would not move. His head went deeper into the mud and he thrashed, kicked with his feet and tried desperately to escape the growing pressure that shoved his head deeper and deeper into the muck.

The claws tore deep into his flesh, peeling his scalp away.

Pulver tried one more time to let out a scream, but no sound escaped past the flesh that was crushing his mouth and shoving his teeth back into his skull. He scrabbled to reach for another grenade, and remembered too late that his hand was no longer there.

� ✕ ✕ ✕

Jermaine Hyde was happiest when he was on the hunt. It wasn't that he liked killing, exactly. It was that he liked the challenge. He wanted to be the best at what he did—something he shared with Hill. He wanted to excel in a field where there were already any number of very good performers.

If he'd been musician, he'd have wanted to be the best. An Eddie Van Halen of the guitar, a Yo-Yo Ma of the cello. Instead, he worked at covert operations and, frankly, assassination. Other members of the Reapers were soldiers, but he never saw himself that way. He was a killer. He'd lie for the reports and say otherwise, but, really, that was what it came down to.

They pointed, he killed.

For this mission, however, the field was different. What he was supposed to kill was bigger, badder, and deadlier than he was. He'd never dealt with something like that.

It was also staggered, and that helped.

He didn't see it when it attacked Pulver. If he had, he'd have done his very best to save the man. Pulver was one of his own, a brother in arms. They fought together and they did it well. Hell, there had been several occasions where Hyde wouldn't have had the chance to make a kill if Pulver hadn't been there to make a big bang loud enough to distract his enemies.

Now Pulver was dead. Tomlin was doing his best to recover from one too many flash-bangs, and Hill was— well, he couldn't see Hill. Maybe the guy was finding an angle of his own for killing the damned alien. He could have it, too, if he beat Hyde to the punch.

Pulver was dead. Something was standing over him and probably dancing a little cabbage patch of celebration, but that didn't matter. What mattered was that Hyde could see the bastard well enough to know it was there.

Hyde's first rule was simple.

If he could see it, he could kill it.

He didn't try for subtle. Instead he pulled his HK45C and fired four rounds into the distortion standing above his friend's corpse. The bullets were black talons. The shells were designed to open up like a flower when they hit a target. Four pieces of metal blossomed outward, each curving and pointed, and tore a target open. Just to add to the fun several small pellets were waiting inside that bloom, suspended in gel. Once fired the bullet spun through a target and then released the pellets into the open wound. Some people called them "sure-kill" rounds. Hyde preferred the term "overkill." Hit a bastard with one of those, and even if it only caught him in the wrist, most of his arm was going away.

Problem was, the bastard he was shooting had protective armor. He saw the ricochet from the first bullet as it hit metal. The second round did the same thing. The third round was higher in the air, and it hit metal, too, but this time the result was different.

The first two rounds staggered the thing. They were .45s and they had a damned fine kick. So bullet one, and the thing splashed in the mud. He imagined it stepping to the side to compensate. Round two and the sound of metal on metal was louder and the thing must have fallen, because there was a bigger splash of mud this time.

Round three, and the shot must have gotten lucky.

The thing's war mask must have taken the brunt. *Bang!* He heard the metal on metal sound again, only this time the alien freak was suddenly visible. He saw the faceplate go sailing sideways as the ugly fucker phased into view in a wash of electrical discharge. The thing's head slapped hard to the left.

The war mask slipped and rolled and then stuck in the mud maybe fifteen feet from where the thing showed up. When the bastard looked his way, the anger in its alien features was impossible to miss.

When it charged him, Hyde felt a tight grin mar his features.

This thing was a killer. This thing was a hunter.

Hyde wanted to prove he was better at both, and now he had his chance.

26

His face throbbed. The attacks had been unexpected and he had become too confident. He was hard to see, not *impossible* to see, and he let his anger get the better of him. The one that had disoriented him had made him angry and he got his revenge, but now he was paying the price for that anger.

He still had both of his eyes. They had broken the lens over one eye, but it had not fragmented the way it could have. Luck was with him on that.

The mask controlled his plasma cannon. He could fire without it, but it would require more work—he would have to manually aim and fire. The targeting lasers were on the mask as well.

He needed to kill these things as quickly as possible.

The one that had knocked aside his war mask aimed at him and fired. As the native fired, he turned his body and covered as much as he could. The weapon was primitive, but powerful. He wore some armor, but not enough to cover all of his body, and he could not assume he would get lucky again.

He was right. A projectile hit the back of his arm where the armor did not protect him and grazed flesh. Had the hit been clean he knew he would have lost his arm. Instead a divot of flesh and muscle was blown away. The pain was immediate and intense.

He roared and threw a disc blade. As the thing did its best to avoid the weapon, he opened the control panel on his gauntlet and tried to re-engage the cloak. This gauntlet was old, but it worked. He saw the shimmer of energies that meant he was once again camouflaged.

By the time he looked up, the one that had fired at him was gone. It had fled, or hidden itself away while he was momentarily occupied.

There were three of them. He needed to eliminate them as quickly as possible.

Two of them were still in his sight.

N N N

Hill shook his head and told himself to stop seeing double.

Concussion. He knew that was the problem as sure as he knew how to count to ten on his fingers and thumbs. The damn medic working on him earlier had said it was possible, and he'd been right.

That didn't mean a thing. There was a mission and he would see it through.

Pulling himself out of the ruins of a carnival game, he was looking right at the monster when it vanished. For half a heartbeat he thought it was his eyes, and then he remembered the thing was good at disappearing. Rather than wait for another chance he aimed and fired where it had been. He didn't hit and cursed his faulty vision.

The thing wasn't gone, though. It was just hiding.

That was a problem because he didn't have that luxury.

Tomlin moved out from behind one of the stands and fired two rounds at the air. The air didn't respond.

"You want to tell me where the hell that thing is hiding?" Tomlin called out loud and clear, and Hill wondered when he'd lost his mind. He was about to respond when he saw motion off to his left.

The mask.

The thing that the alien had been wearing was sitting in the mud, and then it wasn't. It rose from its spot and floated to a height of about four feet.

There was no part of Devon Hill that believed in ghosts. If he had, he'd have quit his line of work a long time ago. He closed one eye and sighted down the barrel of his pistol, and then he fired—and he got lucky. The mask stayed in the air but it moved about a foot to the left and green blood blew across the air and spilled down into the water flowing across the muddy ground.

He fired again, and a third time, aiming at the bloody patch.

The mask rose up again and then it vanished. He could almost imagine that ugly bastard putting the steel face back over that disgusting visage. In his mind's eye, he could see where the mask had faded behind whatever cloaking tech it was using.

Hill tried aiming again, and only hit the mud.

Then he moved, because at that moment he was probably the best target the thing had, and he didn't particularly want to die.

It was a wise choice. One of those damned throwing discs glimmered into sight at high speed and came right for him. If he hadn't been in motion it probably would have caught him in the chest. Instead it only jammed into his left hand and sank through bone and flesh alike.

Hill hissed and stared down at the blades piercing his flesh. His vision swam a bit as he moved around the side of the House of Mirrors and leaned against the wall. The blades were deep and there was no way in hell he was leaving them in place. He gritted his teeth and pulled. The advantage to sharp blades was they came out easily, especially when there were no barbs involved. The blood spilled out easily, too, until he pulled the kerchief from the back left pocket of his pants and wrapped it tightly around his hand.

Automatic fire chattered through the rain. That'd be Tomlin.

He hoped the man found his target.

Rather than waiting on the sidelines to find out, Hill moved back onto the fairground and looked for himself. He closed an eye again to make sure he only saw one of everything. Tomlin was crouching and taking careful aim. He squeezed the trigger and a dozen bullets cut the air apart before at least one or two of them hit a target.

The alien let out another scream, and an instant later Tomlin echoed the sound. He rose into the air even as his M-16 sailed out of his hands. Tomlin kicked out and his foot hit something solid, but it barely seemed to have any impact. A second kick had the same result.

But seeing him hit something meant that Hill had a target.

Two rounds. Both of them hit something.

Tomlin dropped into the mud and rolled, coughing, his face dark.

Hill fired two more rounds. His clip was almost empty and he'd need to change it out soon, but in the meantime he was fairly certain he'd hit something again. Then a trio of pinpoints of light squared themselves on his chest. He knew he was fucked, then the flare of blue light came at him.

Hill did the only thing he could think of.

He dropped straight down.

The wall behind him was vaporized. Flinders of wood flew in every direction, peppered him with splinters, and sent something hot and burning into his eye. The pain in his hand was nothing in comparison.

Hill let out a whimper and closed the eye, resisting the urge to press his palm into the wound. Hot fluids ran down his cheek and mingled with the rain and he didn't dare touch it, not if he hoped to keep his eye when it was all said and done.

The alien fired at him again and he crawled on his hands and knees, and then rolled to try to avoid being shot. The second round was wild, maybe meant to flush him out. The House of Mirrors collapsed in on itself and he was up and running, his feet doing their best to slide in the mud despite his wishes.

"Motherfucker's going down." He meant it, too. He was in pain and he was angry, and he still wanted payback for Pappy and the rest.

Shuffling around the side of a series of porta-potties he ran the distance behind them, cursing and scowling and wishing he could get a clean shot at the damn thing that was hiding away instead of actually fighting.

✄ ✄ ✄

Tomlin coughed and sucked in air. His throat felt like he'd been caught in a noose—which really was about what had happened. The damned thing had picked him up by the neck and shaken him like a rag doll and there wasn't a damned thing he could do about it.

He'd tried finding the elbow of the massive arm and failed. He'd tried kicking the thing and he definitely hit something, but it was like kicking a stone wall. Nothing he did had any effect on the alien bastard. His rifle was gone and his pistol was missing—he had no idea where the hell it had sailed off to. He wasn't weaponless exactly, but he was down to a KA-BAR knife. A damned fine weapon, but it surely felt too small when he slipped it into his hand.

An explosion of light flashed through the air from ten feet to his left, and Tomlin watched one of the structures blow into shreds. Another burst, and while he was watching he duckwalked through the mud and drove the blade of his knife up into flesh that he only saw as a slight distortion in the air. The blade went in deep and he took advantage of that, pulling the weapon through the trapped flesh and sawing as hard as he could.

Maybe he'd get lucky and cripple the bastard.

The flesh he was cutting moved, and an instant later something slammed into his face with enough force to send him sliding through the mud, still gripping the knife and trying to remember his name. Looking where his enemy had been, he saw the footprints coming for him as they slapped mud out of the way.

Tomlin measured the distance and calculated the center mass of the thing headed his way, doing complex mathematics without even being aware of it. Then he reversed the blade in his hand and hurled it toward what he suspected was the stomach of his enemy.

The blade slammed hard into something and quivered in the air.

He stood up and followed it, not giving himself time to think. He'd wounded it, and he needed this thing down. He could see the trail of luminescent green that spilled into the muck behind those eerie empty footsteps.

Searing pain scraped across his ribs as he smashed into a wall of hidden flesh. Two separate lines of fire crawled along his side and stole his breath away. His body came to a complete stop and he grunted. An inch in the wrong direction and he had no doubt those blades would have punched through his armor and his ribs with the same ease. The Kevlar never had a chance against them.

The knife was still there. Whatever sort of energies the creature used to cloak itself, the blade had fallen victim to them and he could see the shape, but not see the weapon.

He didn't care. His hand grabbed the hilt, felt the familiar grip, and he sawed again as he tore the blade free.

The second time around the nightmare's blades caught on his vest, and Tomlin was flung through the air as it tried to shake its weapons free of the obstruction. He flipped half a circle and then crashed down, sliding through the heavy running water and crashing into one of the massive oil drums that had been set up as a trash bin. His head rang, and his vision went white for an instant.

It was coming for him again, and it was moving quickly. The splashes that disrupted the mud were strong enough to rise almost a yard into the air, giving him a clear picture of where the thing was, despite its ability to hide in plain sight.

Tomlin dropped into a combat stance and readied himself. If the thing decided to fight him instead of just blowing him into dust, he still had a chance, and so far it seemed determined to give him that opportunity.

Five strides away and he could just make out the basic shape through the pouring rain. Four strides and it was clearer, but still distorted air, no details to be seen. Three steps and he could make out the shape of the legs, the arms, could almost count the fingers. There were two long lines of distortion that looked like they might be the blades that had chopped his armor into shreds.

Two strides and he was moving, driving forward with all of his strength, pushing the blade at the center of the mass coming for him.

One stride and the damned thing hit him like a hurricane. Tomlin was lifted off his feet and sent rolling through the air. He'd been hit damned good, too, because as much as he wished otherwise he could feel where the blades on the thing's right arm had cut into his abdomen.

His blade stayed where it was, yanked from his hand by the force of impact. There was a very real chance that his wrist was broken but he couldn't concentrate past the hammering pain in his guts and the spill of hot liquids across his belly. He was likely as good as dead. His body just hadn't caught that clue yet.

The alien didn't seem to care. Tomlin fell to his knees and tried to convince his body to move. His eyes looked where the thing had been just a moment before and he saw it well enough in the torrential rain—a ghost that was exactly solid enough to have water splash off of its body.

The ghost came for him again.

27

The knife had cut deep into muscle, not once, but twice. It was long enough to leave him worried about whether or not his internal organs had been cut, but there was no time to consider that. There were still two more of the creatures hunting him—that he knew of—and they were better armed than this one.

Quickly he scanned the area, looking for traces of the two, but if they were near they were hiding behind the various obstacles. They had chosen well, limiting his advantage, and he didn't trust climbing again on the chance that more of their explosive devices were within easy reach.

With only one target in sight, he charged the creature he had just wounded. It held one arm over its abdomen and he could see the blood flowing from it into the muddy waters. If he were a cruel hunter he might have left it alone to suffer and die, but he could be merciful when the need arose. He was not a sadist. He was a hunter. There was a difference.

While he was contemplating the death of his prey, one of the others shot him again. The impact was tremendous. He staggered back and then hit the ground, rolling in the warm muck. His left calf had been hit, and his armor kept the limb intact, but the pain was bone-numbing and he suspected the guard he wore had been dented.

He looked around and saw his assailant. It tried to dodge behind a structure before he could see it, but was too slow.

He did not rise, but instead stayed low to the ground and crawled. They could see him in the rain and he knew that, but if they were looking higher up they might miss seeing him as he moved.

His wounds were bad enough that he was concerned. Still, he could not leave behind the objects these creatures had taken from him, could not let them have the technology. It went against the directives of his people. So he continued the hunt, and he hunted more carefully than before. If he failed to rectify the situation the penalty would be grim.

He crawled around the side of the obstacle, expecting to find his prey, but when he arrived the one that had shot him was no longer where he anticipated.

N N N

Hyde looked down from his position on the Ferris wheel and frowned. Maybe the damned thing was coming toward where he'd been, and maybe it wasn't. Hard to say. There was a spread of the green blood in the muck, but only a small amount. Could have been bled off from somewhere else, and he didn't know if he wanted to waste a bullet on maybe.

He had four bullets left and one spare clip. That sounded like a lot, but it wasn't—not when the fucking thing refused to die.

So he waited.

Just to let him know how stupid that idea was, a volley of electrical blasts ripped across the horizon and lit him up where he was standing. If anyone or anything was looking up, they'd spot him in an instant. He was a good target for the lightning, too.

"Screw it." He squeezed off a round and saw the mud explode. If there was something there, he'd missed it. So Hyde started back down from the Ferris wheel. Wherever the thing was hiding, he'd have to shoot it from ground level.

The climb up to his perch had been treacherous in the tempest, and the path down was just as risky. The winds were bad enough that the ride rocked on its foundation, and they were picking up. Did he think it was going to fall over? No.

But he still felt more comfortable when he was back on the muddy ground.

Hyde moved quickly toward where he'd seen the green trail of blood, but the waters had washed it away, leaving no trace or any sort of trail. He was extra alert as he moved away from the spot—he'd let himself be seen, and now he had to wait for a response.

He didn't have to wait long.

The catch was not to look for anything at all. He left

his eyes unfocused and moved slowly to alter his field of vision. Off to his left Devon Hill was moving carefully along the side of "Madam Marissa's Fortunes." The tent was leaning perilously, and he guessed it would be a goner before the hunt was over.

Tomlin was in the same spot as where he'd fallen. Not dead, but hurt bad. He was shaking hard. Looked like Hill was heading in his direction. Part of him wanted to do the same thing. Tomlin was his commanding officer. He was also a friend, but Hyde knew if he took time away from the hunt, Tomlin would be pissed off. They had a mission, and he needed to finish it.

There. To his right.

The movement was small, subtle, and if he'd been focused on looking, he would have missed it. Instead he damn near sensed the change and when he looked— really looked—he saw the distortion field that marked where the thing stood.

It was maybe thirty feet away from Tomlin, and it was waiting for Hill to get there. The bastard was heading right for it.

Rather than call out, Hyde took aim and squeezed off two rounds. At least one of them hit. The thing stepped back and spun hard to the right. There was another noise of metal on metal, barely even a tinkle in the torrential rain, and then the alien roared and charged for him. Any and every chance of stealth was gone, but at least the damned thing hadn't thrown one of those nasty-ass blades at him. Not yet.

He still had trouble seeing where it was. The waters

splashed where feet hit the ground, but it moved so damned fast. All Hyde could do was watch as it thundered his way, and then duck when the time came.

As a huge arm swept toward him, he dodged left and lowered his body into a crouch. It was moving fast and would have to get rid of the momentum before it could turn and try for him a second time.

Looked good on paper, but the thing swept an arm back as it moved, and smacked him across the side of his head. It wasn't a fatal blow but it hurt like hell and Hyde spilled into the muck, then rolled back to his feet, wobbling more than he wanted to think about. While he was trying to catch his balance, the fucker kicked him in his side.

The blow wasn't perfect. Again, if it had been, he would have been out of commission. Instead of knocking his ribs into a new shape it only sent him reeling a second time and trying to compensate for the kinetic force of the hit.

The thing didn't intend to let him recover. It came straight at him, and that was fine with Hyde. He didn't intend to let it off easy, either.

When it came around this time, swinging one thick arm that he could barely distinguish from the air, Hyde braced, blocked, and then pivoted on the hip while holding that limb. Jiu-jitsu was all about throws and blocks and using an enemy's force against them. He threw the bastard a couple of feet through the air, feeling every ounce of his enemy as he finished the move.

The alien hit the ground hard, making an epic splash. Rather than let go, Hyde moved his hands up the wrist and captured the thumb on that hand. Funny thing about fingers and thumbs—as tough as the bones were, the joints could be surprisingly weak. He dislocated the thumb with a hard twist and then backed away as the creature let out a roar of fury, or maybe just pain.

It came up in an explosion of dirty water and charged for him again. He could try to throw it, but it wasn't going to do much good if the thing wasn't swinging. This time around it wasn't off balance, and it clocked him full on, knocking him into the flooding waters without so much as trying.

This time the blow was too solid for him to brush off.

Mostly transparent or not, he saw the big-ass blades pop on that wrist gauntlet. Hyde moved, pushing himself through the muck and avoiding the first blow. The second was better timed and the blades carved through his vest. They narrowly missed taking a part of his chest along for the ride. The third swipe caught on his helmet and tore it free from his head, neatly scraping his left ear off in the process. The pain was intense enough that he guessed the cartilage had been torn.

He'd have been dead right then if Hill hadn't stepped in and taken a shot.

N N N

Fury was overwhelming him. The creature was half his size, and it kept eluding him, kept hurting him. He didn't want to let anger get the best of him, but felt himself drowning in a tide of emotions just the same.

The war mask wasn't helping. He'd hoped that the enhanced vision—even with just one lens—would be enough, but instead he was moving around half blind, and he couldn't do it any longer. He needed to see properly if he was going to kill his prey.

Finally the thing was caught. He hit it hard enough that it fell, and he saw blood spilling down the side of its head where one of the small, soft curls of the ear had been torn away.

It looked around, clearly disoriented.

Abruptly there was an impact as solid as a strike to the face. One of the other life forms had shot him. His war mask rang out again, and this time when it slid sideways he ripped it down and cast it aside. Putting it back on had been a mistake. Best to trust his senses.

Turning, he saw the thing where it stood. It saw him, as well, despite the cloak, and it fired again. The missile cut across his throat and hit hard enough to make him cough, but did not penetrate. He staggered and reached for his gauntlet.

A moment later the cannon shifted in his shoulder. Four hard bursts of plasma erupted from it and lit the darkness. Explosion after explosion tore the ground apart, leaving smoking craters in their wake. He didn't care if he hit his enemy. He cared that it stopped shooting at him, and in that he was successful. The thing screeched and ran and was hurled through the air.

When the debris settled, the three creatures remained. All of them were injured, but not one of them had yet died.

He needed to revise that as quickly as he could.

28

"Sheriff?" Laney's voice on the radio always sounded like she was trying to imitate Marilyn Monroe. Sultry, sexy, and silky. It would have had more of an impact on Sheriff Tom Lauder if he wasn't happily married, and if Laney didn't bear an unsettling resemblance to his brother-in-law Mike.

Mike was nice and all, but not exactly a sexy thing in his estimation. And both Mike and Laney could have lost a spare tire without it causing them any harm.

"Yeah, Laney?" he responded. "What blew up this time?" The storm was a bear, and it was knocking the bejesus out of everything in the county without even trying. In a perfect world he would have been at home, eating a plate of his wife's spaghetti with meatballs and watching *Survivor*. Instead he was driving down State Road 11 and making sure the flooding hadn't washed out any of the small bridges along this stretch of his territory.

"Nothing blew up, Sheriff, but there have been complaints of shots fired down at the fairground."

Tom frowned. "Isn't the Hartshorn Carnival closed down due to the storm? Smart move. I think Bill Hartshorn said he wanted to skip that sort of liability."

"It is, and he did, but somebody's out there firing weapons."

In the seat next to him Deputy Annie Traynor was frowning. Her expression said exactly what he was thinking—if some redneck dumbass was out there drunk and shooting the hell out of the carnival, there was going to be a major problem. The paperwork for vandalism on that level was a pain in the ass.

"We're on it." He paused for a moment. "Know what, Laney?"

"What's that, Sheriff?"

"I'd like you to call Phil and Andy over here, too. Just in case we've got another incident with a bike club."

Whoever had destroyed the Four Horsemen Bike Club, and killed at least half the charter members, had done a helluva job. He'd never seen that much blood. It wasn't close to solved, and the bikers, as friendly as they could be and as nice as they were when it came to doing their civic duties, also dealt with drugs and other illegal substances. It seemed to him like some sort of sick vendetta.

On top of the killings, the cancellation of their annual Biker Week had gone badly. So far four different groups who'd come into town to have a good time had started drunken brawls, or tried their hand at arson, or fired off a few hundred rounds at the empty garage that sat next to the Four Horsemen clubhouse.

It's all fun and games until someone gets drunk and decides to let loose.

"I'll have them meet you there, Sheriff."

"You're a doll, Laney," he said. "Thank you."

She giggled and killed the radio chatter.

Annie looked at him, rolled her eyes, and then made a gagging noise.

"What?"

"'You're a doll, Laney,'" she said. "'Thank you, Laney.'" Her imitation of him was an octave too high but otherwise pretty good.

"What was I supposed to say?"

"I don't know, maybe just leave it at thank you, without the flirting?"

"Honey and vinegar," he said. "I flirt with Laney and the world is a better place. I don't flirt with Laney and she forgets to give me my messages when I get to the office."

"So you're a john?"

"When it comes to getting my phone messages, yes I am."

She chuckled and shook her head. "I'm telling your wife."

"Oh, she knows."

"I bet she does."

"I take out the trash on Friday, we have sex on Saturday," he replied without a hint of irony. "I do my chores, and I am handsomely rewarded."

"That's so much more than I ever needed to know about you, Tom."

"You know you like it."

She made another retching sound as they passed the helicopter parked on the clearing at the edge of the carnival. The cruiser slewed sideways as Tom hit the brakes, and then Annie opened her window to the rain and aimed a flashlight at the black aircraft.

"Seriously?" She looked at the bird and shook her head. "What, bikers with guns aren't enough? Now we're having them imported?"

Tom didn't even bother with the flashers. A few seconds later they were out and soaking wet. There was a man sitting in the pilot seat of the copter, staring at them as they came closer. He opened the door.

"Want to explain this one, friend?" Tom looked at the man. He was dressed in black pants and a black t-shirt. He held out his credentials and Tom read them, not really caring. He just wanted answers.

"Just waiting for my clients to come back." That was about as carefully neutral a face as he'd ever seen, and Annie shook her head, sending a spray off the wide-brimmed hat that was keeping her face mostly dry. As calm as the guy was acting, he seemed mighty nervous.

"Clients?" he echoed.

"Yes, Sheriff. They said they came down here to assess some property?"

"In the middle of this?"

"It wasn't this bad when I landed."

"When was that, last week?"

The man gave a mild, polite chuckle that didn't sound real. "I have to make a living. The winds weren't so bad, and I could charge them extra, so I figured why not?"

"Just be careful when you leave," Lauder said. "This gets any worse and I'll ground you myself." He wasn't sure he could do that, but the pilot probably didn't know that.

"I'm very seriously considering calling an Uber and telling them to go to hell when they get done."

"Yeah? That might be a good idea. You might not get rich, but you'd be alive."

The pilot nodded his head. "Amen, brother."

"That's Sheriff Brother to you." He said the words without venom. It was Florida. Stranger things happened every day. He took a picture of the call letters on the side of the bird and made a mental note to run them when the night was done. If the man was legit he was fine. If he thought there was drug business going on, it was going to be a bad day for someone. He didn't expect drugs, though. The guy looked too clean for that sort of crap.

Back in the car he shook his head again and looked over to Annie. "Can you believe this? Every damned time I think I've seen everything—"

That was when the explosions rocked the night from the direction of the carnival. He hit the flashers and Annie started calling it in even as Tom gunned the cruiser forward.

It was going to be a longer night than they'd thought.

N N N

Devon Hill crawled back to his feet and shook the mud from the side of his face. He was alive and he was pissed off. Fucking crab-faced bastard had all the advantages. It was gone again, of course. At least he got it off Hyde before it could kill the man.

That was something.

When the blue flashing lights came around the side of the Ferris wheel, no one was more surprised. The cop car came to a halt and two shapes got out of it. Both of them carried flashlights and looked as if they meant business—at least as much as Hill could tell. One of them was staring right at him and walking in his direction.

"You want to leave." He shook his head and squinted in the glare from the vehicle. "It's not safe here."

"Well, I think we might be better judges of that. What the *hell* is going on here, anyway?" The woman's voice threw him. He was so used to being around men in uniform. That, or maybe that last blast from the enemy had rattled his brains more than he wanted to think about.

"There's a situation here," he said, glancing around the entire time. "You need to leave. I can't explain. It's dangerous."

She pulled a pistol. It looked like a toy in her hand.

"You need to put your hands up in the air. You need to stay exactly where you are." That was when he remembered that he was holding a weapon in his own hand.

"No. Wait. This doesn't have to get ugly. I'm warning you—"

"Drop the weapon and put your hands above your head, friend." That voice came from the other uniform. He had a hand on the radio attached to his shoulder.

"I'll drop the weapon! I'll drop the weapon!" Hill wanted them gone and he wanted them alive. This wasn't part of their day, part of their world, and he needed to keep it that way. "Just, please, lower your weapons and leave. This is a serious situation, and you are in danger."

"Son, you have no idea how serious it is."

You did not just call me son. "Listen, this is… it's a covert operation. This is a very dangerous spot, and there are already several injured parties."

"Get down on the ground!" the woman shouted at him. "Hands above your head. This is over *now*."

Hill started to lower to the ground when the woman's head exploded.

The sheriff turned fast, his eyes wide.

"Annie!" He turned back toward Hill, waving his gun like an amateur, and then looked around, but there was nothing to see.

The man reached for his radio.

Hill rose and tried for him. There was no choice—he was about to call for backup, and if that happened the clusterfuck would only get worse. There was still a very small chance they could contain this situation, but it was getting smaller by the second.

The sheriff was faster than he expected. "Officer down! Repeat, I have an officer down at the carnival!"

It was all gone to hell, just that fast.

There would be no pulling the locals back.

The sheriff had his service pistol pointed directly at Hill. And then he went sailing backward, his eyes wide and a thick arm around his throat.

Hyde dropped him fast, but not quite fast enough. In the distance they could hear another cop siren. Hyde hit the sheriff in the side of his head three times. It didn't kill the man, but he wasn't going to get back up any time soon.

Leaning over, he took the service piece.

"We have to end this."

Hill nodded.

"End this." The words came from behind Hill and he spun quickly, looking for the source. He saw nothing, but he felt the creature's hands grab his throat and his crotch, lift him like he was nothing, and hurl him through the air. He slammed into Hyde hard enough to send them both into the water and mud again.

They rolled and slipped and grunted, and Hill felt that damn dizziness come back to shake his senses. Hyde stood up and backed away, looking for their target. He opened fire with the pistol in his hand and hit something.

At the same time, one of the round blades slammed into Hill's head. The curved tines drove through flesh and into bone, breaking open his sinuses and quivering in the side of his face. The impact was great enough that he went down, and hard, fading from consciousness even as he became aware of the pain.

N N N

Hyde shook his head. Everything hurt and it wasn't getting any better.

The damned thing was tougher than it had any right to be, and he wanted it dead before it could prove that fact again. Then it killed Hill. One throw and the man dropped like a freshly cut tree.

He fired again and scored a major hit. Something went wrong with the cloaking device and the creature came back into focus in all its hideous glory.

It was looking worse for wear. Several wounds were obvious now, bullet holes that had carved pieces of the hideous thing away. It bled from the chest, from the abdomen, from the left leg and from both arms. There were abrasions running along the side of the thing's monstrous face.

It looked directly at Hyde and those deadly blades popped from the right gauntlet. The eyes of the creature rolled, and it opened its mouth wide as it roared another challenge. Hyde backed up and crouched even as the lights came around the corner.

The Sheriff's Department was on the roll. There was a new squad car present and, much as he agreed with Hill and wished that civilians could have stayed away, he was grateful for the distraction.

The monster looked toward the vehicle and stormed in that direction.

Hyde let it go.

Hill let out a snort of pain and his face twisted into an ugly mask. He was still alive. Him and Tomlin both, but they weren't going to be around much longer.

The radio piece on his collar was muddied and soaked, but Hyde checked to see if it still worked. They'd used it person-to-person, and he opened up an outside frequency.

"We've got a bird out here. Who's flying it?"

He'd seen the helicopter. They'd followed it, and if he was lucky the pilot might still be in the area.

As he tried, the alien moved to the cop car and roared another challenge. The driver hadn't come to a complete halt yet, but he did exactly what Hyde wouldn't have done. He slammed the vehicle into reverse and tried to get away from the inhuman thing charging toward him.

The creature charged after the car and then stopped and braced. A moment later another blast of energy ripped from that damned shoulder cannon and blew the right front side of the engine into shreds.

Someone answered him on the radio.

"It's Rodriguez. Who is this?" The voice was almost challenging.

"This is Hyde of the Reapers. We have people down and need them extracted."

"The Reapers? Aren't you under quarantine?"

"Not with that thing loose. Your team is gone, every last one of them. Get your ass over here and help me extract my survivors."

He could just see Rodriguez doing the math. The guy had been ordered to stay put—otherwise he would've been there long ago. Hyde had no authority over him, but he had a very serious reputation as a killer.

He decided to play on his rep.

"Don't piss me off, Rodriguez," he growled. "I have a thing to finish killing."

The pilot let out a stream of Hispanic obscenities.

That was all the time Hyde had. The alien had ripped off the driver's side door and was peeling one of the cops from the damaged car. The guy was already bleeding, and he screamed as the creature looked him in the face.

Hyde limped in closer as carefully as he could. The deputy started fighting, doing his best, but the man was seriously outclassed.

The other side of the car opened and another deputy came out shooting. The first bullet hit the alien in the arm. The second bullet hit the deputy dangling in the creature's hand. Whether or not it killed him, Hyde could not say, but the guy went silent. All he knew for certain was that the damned thing was ignoring him for a few more seconds.

That was all the time he needed.

Three steps closer and the creature turned, looking down at him.

He'd have preferred to hit it from behind.

From four feet away he unloaded the sheriff's SIG Sauer P226 into the alien's chest. It staggered backward, eyes closed in pain as bullet after bullet tore through the meat and bone and exited through the back of the damned beast.

It should have dropped. It should have died.

The blades came around in a savage arc and though he tried, Hyde couldn't elude them. He was simply too close.

Jermaine Hyde went down hard. Only the certainty that he had killed the alien would help him into whatever afterlife might have awaited.

29

He was dying. He had killed the last of the things that hunted him; the other two were dying if not already dead. He was dying and now he had two choices—leave, or stay and destroy his property.

One of the new creatures came for him, firing its weapon. He threw his disc again and watched as the thing fell into separate parts.

He had to leave. If he could make his ship he could still get home. He could still mend. He could find all of his weapons and manage to hide all evidence that he had been here.

The wounds in his chest were agony.

He was dying. Dying!

No. He had not come here to die. He had come here to hunt and to gather his trophies. He would return home. He would tell tales of his time here and he would show his new collection proudly.

He ran only a few hundred paces before he collapsed

in the mud. His breaths were a collection of broken, shattered, painful gulps that failed to fill his lungs with even the thin air of the local atmosphere.

Opening the cover on his gauntlet, he stared at the control buttons. The pain crawled through him and made his eyes blur. His eyes, and his thoughts alike.

✽ ✽ ✽

Tomlin stared at the metal spear for a long while as he held his insides in place. He did his best to watch the fight. Sometimes he saw something and other times he faded away.

Dying. He was dying. He knew it. There wasn't a thing for it except to hope that the others finished the job and killed the alien hunter.

If he'd been able to catch a breath he would have cheered when Hyde blew the back out of the alien. He'd have cried when the alien cut Hyde's face in half and split him most of the way down to his crotch, too.

The police showed up, and then they died.

Hill was down. He was probably dead, too.

The damned alien was moving. It started to run toward the south, toward the Okefenokee, and then it fell flat. He watched as it crawled a few feet, wheezing and coughing and feeling almost as shitty as he did. He didn't want to cheer anymore. He just wanted it to be over.

It looked like the only one who was going to end all of this was him.

Tomlin made it to his knees. It was hard, damn it. It was maybe the hardest thing he'd ever done in his entire life, and then he looked down at that damned alien spear again. He reached out, let his hand touch it.

The metal was cold and it was surprisingly light. He pulled it closer and stuck the pointy end into the ground. It slid a little before punching into the soil and staying put.

One hand stayed on his stomach—he was almost certain that if he let that hand fall away, his guts were going to slop on out and spill all over the ground. If that happened, friends and neighbors, he was damn sure he'd never pull them back into his body before he died.

It took an eternity to stand up. During that time the rain fell, and lightning flashed, and thunder crashed. A few million raindrops hit his face and body. Still, he persisted. It was important that he get all the way to his feet, though he was having trouble remembering why.

There was something he had to do. Something important, too, because if he didn't do it, he was pretty sure Pappy was going to yell at him. Sure, Pappy was dead and he knew that, but it didn't matter. Pappy would be pissed off and an angry Pappy was never a good thing.

Another flash of lightning, and then he saw the alien where it lay. It was moving something on its arm and waving long taloned fingers over that spot. Something Pappy had said about the aliens buzzed in his head, and he tried to focus.

"Oh. Shit. Bomb." He shook his head. "No, no, no, no…" Tomlin moved. It wasn't exactly his best time. He was moving slower than his granddaddy when he was using his walker, but he was moving and that was the part that mattered.

He headed for the alien and—

N N N

When he could think again he was looking down at the mud and most of his weight was leaning on the spear that he'd been using to hold him upright. By some miracle his hand was still holding his insides where they belonged, and it didn't look like anything important had leaked out, but he could feel too much warmth running down his abdomen and his crotch.

"Shit." He barely heard himself speak.

The alien was still there. It wasn't moving much but it was still there. That had to count.

He moved forward again, trying to remember what was going on, what he had to do. It was important. He knew that. He knew the alien was part of it. The damned thing was panting and shaking. It was dying, he was sure of it, and he felt a surge of savage joy at the idea. That would show it not to mess with the Reapers.

Tomlin uttered a barely sane laugh as he moved closer to the hunter. The faceplate of its gauntlet was open and red characters were flashing down. A series of beeps came from the thing, each one a tiny bit louder, just a touch faster.

Tomlin stared and stared, uncertain what he should do or why the noises were making him nervous. He was nervous, no two ways about it. There was something important about it.

His anger was sudden and irrational but he ran with it. Though it hurt him to do so, he lifted the spear with both hands and drove it down into the shifting characters on the gauntlet. There was a heavy electrical discharge and the flashing lights stopped.

"That'll show you."

The words were slurred and barely coherent. Something wet happened along the front of his uniform and Tomlin looked down to see parts of him falling toward the running water and puddles below.

"What the hell did you do, Tomlin?"

He didn't recognize the voice. A hand caught him as he started to fall backward. The world crashed into darkness.

30

Rodriguez found the corpses. Lots of corpses. The men who'd come with him were toast. Every last one of them. Some of them had been pulled apart or skinned or both. A few were missing their heads.

He didn't worry about the dead. The fact was that corpses were easier to make disappear than live people. The locals might wonder what happened to a body or two, but they'd shut up and ignore them if the right pressure was applied—and there were people working for Stargazer who knew what sort of pressure to apply.

Living witnesses were a different situation, and to that end he collected what was left of Tomlin and carried him to the copter as fast as he could, horrified by what was trying to spill out of his stomach. Tomlin made noises. He groaned and he whimpered and a few times he almost made coherent words, but mostly he just made noises.

Hill cursed up a blue streak as Rodriguez helped him back to the helicopter. His face was swollen and the thing sticking out of his skull shivered with every step they took, but it stayed where it was. The man was feverish, and he could understand that.

The alien thing was dead. No two ways around that. It was dead when he pulled Tomlin away and it was dead when he came back around. He tried to pull it toward the helicopter and quickly gave up. He was a strong man, but no way in hell he was moving that thing.

Hyde was dead. He found the poor bastard as he headed back for the copter one last time. By that point more emergency vehicles were coming. He'd known there was going to be a problem when the sheriff played twenty questions.

The storms were worse than ever by the time he got the rotors moving, and there was no choice but to go up into the storm. No choice at all, because if the cops found him there would be questions that he wasn't supposed to answer.

The winds did their best to knock his ass into the trees and then into the Ferris wheel and then into the ground. Below him he saw five cop cars and at least two ambulances heading for the fairground. They were definitely in for an unpleasant surprise.

The body of the alien was a problem.

They couldn't be allowed to see that. It was too damning and too controversial. But what could he do about it?

Rodriguez wanted to call the home base and warn them, but that would be foolish in the extreme. The radio frequency was supposed to be secure, but he knew that was about as accurate as saying the moon was made of cheese. Someone somewhere would always be listening in. The conversations could be coded, they could be conducted in a make-believe language, but someone somewhere would be listening and would crack the code.

He'd made it up to four hundred feet when the winds fought for control of the helicopter and almost won. It was while he was fighting to regain control of the bird that the skies behind him suddenly lit up with the most violent explosion he'd ever seen.

Holy shit!

"Night became day." He'd heard the statement before, and understood the notion, but for a few seconds it became reality. The light was so bright that he was nearly blinded. A loud squawk of feedback came over his radio and did its best to deafen him. A moment later the copter shuddered and jerked as a massive wind hit it hard enough to send him into a spin.

He pulled out, but just barely, and headed back for the base.

Rodriguez did a lot of work in covert operations. He didn't fight the good fight. He didn't fight the bad fight. He flew into areas where he wasn't supposed to be, and he flew back out of them with no one the wiser. He'd taken flights through war zones. He'd safely made his way through jungles while flying twenty feet above the trees and dodging bullets. He was, in short, a damned fine pilot.

When all was said and done, Rodriguez had pulled out two of the Reapers and left the area. He could verify that the Predator was dead when he took off. That was *all* he could verify, though.

Traeger wouldn't be thrilled. The general wouldn't be happy, either, but they still had some of their new toys and it was possible they would find the alien's ship. All that anyone knew for certain was that it was likely close to where the carnival had been located.

The carnival that was gone. And Rodriguez was good with that, too. Because he'd made it away and all the evidence of what had gone down had been destroyed.

He called that a win.

� ✶ ✶

William Traeger was not happy.

On the one hand, yes, he was delighted. He was now in charge of Project Stargazer. That one went in the win column. There was evidence to support the existence of the otherworldly life form. Big plus. That was another win.

The Predator was missing and presumed dead. Okay, that sucked, but it was what it was.

The Reapers were dead. Most of them at any rate.

He looked over at the general where he sat with his two remaining men. They were both in medically induced comas while their bodies tried to heal from the severe damage inflicted by the Predator.

The old man talked to them every day. He filled them in on the latest news as if they could hear every word. Maybe they could. Traeger had never been in a coma, and figured he'd try to avoid that particular experience for as long as he could.

Woodhurst was just being a good little soldier. In the four weeks that had passed since the Predator had escaped and caused all kinds of damage, the man had proven efficient and loyal. He had a passion for the program, and that went a long way.

The explosion that took out the fairground destroyed a small portion of Deer Water Springs, Florida, as well. According to Miguel Rodriguez, the Predator's control gauntlet had been damaged. There was a spear stuck through it. It must have still done its job, though.

That was a blessing. A damned fine blessing. The explosion was big, but small enough that they could conceal it and say that the local levee had failed, leading to the floods that wiped out part of the town and the surrounding area. All thanks to a screw-up on the part of the Corps of Engineers—at least that was what the press was told.

And it was true. The levee *had* broken.

A good cover-up was essential in their line of business.

Maybe he was happy after all.

The alien faceplate was being examined very carefully. So far it held its secrets. The wrist gauntlet had been meticulously assessed, and had offered up several sound bites that would have sent Orologas into a fit of ecstasy. There were full conversations recorded on that thing, and Traeger had no doubt that eventually they would crack the language barrier. Several inept linguists were already trying and failing. That pissed him off.

Orologas would have been a better choice, because the man had possessed a passion that bordered on obsession. That was one of the reasons he chose to keep Woodhurst around. The man had a lot of clout in his own right, and he cared about Stargazer. *Really* cared. That kind of passion was difficult to replace.

So Woodhurst got to stay around as long as he played by the rules. Thus far he was playing very nicely. Traeger would watch him and make sure it stayed that way. He could replace the man in a second flat—he already had a list of candidates lined up. But better the devil you know, and he knew Woodhurst well enough to keep him satisfied. Though on a short leash.

Church came over with a clipboard full of forms. He looked nervous.

"Got the latest papers for you."

"Anything good?"

"There's the possibility that a transmission got out."

"Come again?"

Church just stared at him, then replied, "Might be that the Predator we dealt with got a transmission out to his people. Maybe a warning that things went wrong." Traeger gave him the stink eye and he stepped back, holding up his hands in surrender. "Might be nothing. We don't know. There was a serious electrical discharge when the explosion happened, and some of the guys think that maybe a transmission was masked in that. They're trying to make certain one way or the other, but so far there's no proof of anything but a lot of noise."

Traeger nodded. He'd mention it to the general and see what the man thought about it. For the moment, however, Woodhurst was busy with his boys.

N N N

He'd said all he needed to say. Really, he could have read them a few pages of the local white pages and the two young men on either side of him would have been none the wiser for it. On his left Hill rested in a coma as his body tried to compensate for multiple skull fractures and some serious brain swelling. There were also a few holes punched in him that had become infected. Every day he got better, but it was by miniscule amounts.

Still, Keyes was "guardedly optimistic" about his chances.

On the other side was Tomlin. Sepsis was the criminal in this case. He'd had half of his internal organs literally dragged through the mud while Rodriguez was trying to save him. His body was fighting the worst of the infections, but the pain levels were rough enough that they weren't letting him wake up during the long battle.

"Okay, boys," he said. "That's it for today, time for you to get some rest." He sighed and stood up from the chair where he'd been resting his backside.

"You're going to get better," he added. "I mean that. You're going to get better and we're going to try this again. I know it doesn't seem like it, boys, but I'm proud of you and what you accomplished. You took out that thing—twice. The second time with only half the team up and functioning."

He sighed and looked from Hill to Tomlin. From Tomlin to Hill.

"I'm proud of you. Pappy would be proud. Time to get

better though, so we can show everyone how it's done."

Neither of the soldiers answered him.

He was an optimist. He believed that someday soon they would. Until then he would hold his vigils and he would do something that had been alien to him for a long time.

He would pray.

ACKNOWLEDGMENTS

The author would like to thank Carol Roeder, Nicole Spiegel, and Steve Tzirlin at Twentieth Century Fox for all of their input and assistance, and to thank Nick Landau, Vivian Cheung, Laura Price, Steve Saffel, David Lancett, Hayley Shepherd, Cameron Cornelius, and all of the fine folks at Titan Books for their endless support and help. Thanks especially to Shane Black and Fred Dekker and Jim Thomas and John Thomas for the source and inspiration.

ABOUT THE AUTHOR

James A. Moore is the award-winning author of more than twenty novels, thrillers, dark fantasy, and horror, including *Alien: Sea of Sorrows*, the critically acclaimed *Fireworks*, *Under The Overtree*, *Blood Red*, the Serenity Falls trilogy (featuring his recurring anti-hero, Jonathan Crowley) and his most recent novels, *Blind Shadows*, *Homestead*, and *Seven Forges*.

James contributed the short story "Distressed" to the anthology *Aliens: Bug Hunt*, and has ventured into the realm of Young Adult novels with his new series Subject Seven.

The author cut his teeth in the industry writing for Marvel Comics and authoring more than twenty role-playing supplements for White Wolf Games. He also penned the White Wolf novels *Vampire: House of Secrets* and *Werewolf: Hell-Storm*.

Harry was staring at the floor.

He didn't look to be breathing.

Not far away, Sarah, Burly's old lady, was staring at the far corner, her mouth open in a silent scream, her eyes wide and her fingers pulling her face into a mask of fright. Suddenly she collapsed to the floor in a faint.

That was just a slice of the whole pie. There was more, but he couldn't make sense of it. Ten feet in front of Sarah, Burly was standing on the air, his feet kicking a few inches from the ground. He was a very large man, one of the biggest Andy had ever met, yet he was floating in the air and making grunting noises as his back split open in two places and he vomited blood.

Burly's thick arms swung back and forth as he reached out and tried to convince the air to let go of him. There was a distortion there, a weird warping of the nothing that was holding him, and Andy thought immediately about the possibilities of camouflage. Not the usual stuff, but the kind you might see in top-secret military labs. It was a passing thought and gone an instant later.

Hanscomb let out a scream that he'd been holding inside. It was more like a sigh because, from the looks of things, his lungs were shredded in his barrel chest. Still, by the look on his face, it was a scream.

Then he slid to the ground and flopped bonelessly, a pile of meat.

The gun. Andy had a gun. He just had to use it was all.

Grabbing for it, he almost dropped it, but got a firm grip and pointed at the place just past Burly's body. His hands shook a bit, and he took aim at that distortion in the air, cursing his nerves for betraying his fear.

Ghosts don't die from bullets. That was what he told himself even as he steadied his grip and took careful aim.

He fired, and the air roared.

Not the sound of his pistol, which he knew very well from the range, but the sound of whatever he'd hit. Something wet and green spilled to the ground even as the air moved. The distortion shifted and danced, and an instant later it was lost in the darkness of the gloomy clubhouse.

Andy took the time to see how many of his friends were dead. Near as he could tell it was almost all of them. Danny was down—his back was broken, too, by the looks of it. Something had blown a hole in Landry. Even Suzie was dead. She'd pulled out her knife and there was something green on it.

Ghost blood! It's ghost blood!

But whatever she'd cut, it had cut back and done a much better job. Tom-Tom was face down on the ground, and most of his back was wet and red from the blood that poured out of it.

A few frantic seconds of looking showed nothing of the ghost, and Andy tried to calm himself, to make his eyes stop bouncing around the room and focus. Holding the gun out with one hand, he wheeled himself from room to room. He was still searching when it found him instead.

The hand holding his pistol vanished in a spray of blood and then reappeared, bouncing across the ground. Adrenaline alone kept him from blacking out from the pain and Andy clutched at his wrist, trying to staunch the heavy blood flow that was painting his jeans black. He gagged and leaned over the side of his wheelchair as the vomit forced itself out of him. The pain was sickening.

The distorted air was there again, and this time it was much closer. The shape was vague at best, but it towered over him. Andy looked up and saw the ghost looking back. His world went dark gray, and then black.

✱ ✱ ✱

He came to when he heard the sound of the clubhouse door being knocked aside. Looking around he saw that the bodies had been torn apart. Heads were missing and worse, far worse, had been done to some of the members of the Four Horsemen. He should have been horrified, but all he felt was numb.

Andy stayed where he was, trying to hold the blood inside his body with strength born of desperation. He was dizzy, and the world spun, then faded to gray for a while and only came back again when he heard the sirens outside.

"Ghosts. Goddamned ghosts."

There was a rumble of distant thunder.

✱ ✱ ✱

The rains came with hard, blasting winds, and hot, thick drops of moisture that obscured nearly everything seen through his helmet, and so he took it off for a moment, sampling the thin native air and the indigenous creatures as they came to take away the dead and tend to the wounded.

No one saw him as he stood on elevated ground. He was not that foolish. There were plenty of targets he could have addressed, but now was not the time. He was here for as long as he needed to be, and there was no reason to hunt quickly and risk losing better prey.

Lightning tore across the darkened sky and the rains grew heavier still, prompting several of the local dominant species to run for cover.

Foolish. Only those tending their wounded seemed unimpressed by the rains. He watched as they took away the broken creature that had actually wounded him with its primitive firearm. They were advanced enough to have projectile weapons, and they had traveled short distances into their solar system, but still they could not detect his kind when cloaked.

Nevertheless, they were enjoyable prey, and they had potential.

Flashing lights advertised the approach of still more vehicles and he watched, taking the measure of each creature that arrived, marking it for possible later hunting. Most were in poor shape and unarmed. They had no weapons and looked to others to offer protection. It was difficult to discern the levels of authority, but there was no need to do so. He was not here to compare sociological views with a different culture.

He was here to hunt, and to prove himself. Still, though they were primitive, he saw similarities to his own society. He could not help but note them—it was his role. For at home he had researched the constantly changing anomalies showing up in some of his species. Many believed that they were adaptive mutations caused when so many of his people traveled among the stars. Others